CENTER of GRAVITY

SHAUNTA GRIMES

FEIWEL AND FRIENDS
New York

A FEIWEL AND FRIENDS BOOK
An imprint of Macmillan Publishing Group, LLC
120 Broadway, New York, NY 10271

Our books may be purchased in bulk for promotional, educational, or business use.
Please contact your local bookseller or the Macmillan Corporate and
Premium Sales Department at (800) 221-7945 ext. 5442 or by email
at MacmillanSpecialMarkets@macmillan.com.

Library of Congress Cataloging-in-Publication Data
Names: Grimes, Shaunta, author.
Title: The center of gravity / Shaunta Grimes.
Description: First edition. | New York : Feiwel and Friends, 2020. |
Summary: When thirteen-year-old Tessa's father remarries months after her
mother's death and moves them to California, Tessa must build a new life and
friendships, while fighting a compulsion about missing children.
Identifiers: LCCN 2019018626| ISBN 9781250191861 (hardcover) |
ISBN 9781250191878 (ebook)
Subjects: | CYAC: Remarriage—Fiction. | Moving, Household—Fiction. |
Compulsive behavior—Fiction. | Friendship—Fiction. | Fathers and daughters—
Fiction. | California—Fiction.
Classification: LCC PZ7.1.G7545 Cen 2020 | DDC [Fic]—dc23
LC record available at https://lccn.loc.gov/2019018626

Book design by Carol Ly

Feiwel and Friends logo designed by Filomena Tuosto
First edition, 2020

10 9 8 7 6 5 4 3 2 1

mackids.com

For Jill, who has always been my partner in crime

ONE

If there was an award for the biggest Neo-Maxi-Zoom-Dweebie alive, I would win. They would put the crown on my head.

Just call me Queen Dweebie 1985.

I hitch my backpack higher on my right shoulder, because even I'm not enough of a dork to wear it with both straps. And I try to pretend that my best friend since the beginning of time isn't trying to pretend that she's not really with me.

To be perfectly honest, I don't blame Megan for walking a few steps ahead and not talking to me on the street. I mean, I *am* that kid who carries her milk carton from lunch around with her all afternoon in the same purple backpack that she's had since the fifth grade.

And I have been *that kid* every day for the last three months, two weeks, and four days.

I can't throw my empty milk cartons away.

I can't leave them in my locker after lunch, either.

The idea of putting them (or, more specifically, the missing kids printed on the backs of them) in a metal coffin that smells like thirty years' worth of gym suits and bologna sandwiches makes me sick.

So I just stick them in my backpack, in the little outside mesh pocket. If I put them inside, where at least no one would see, my books will squish them.

I learned that the hard way.

So from fifth period through the bus ride home, an old, empty milk carton is just *there* for every kid at Pine View Middle School to see. Once wouldn't have mattered. But every day for three months, two weeks, and four days, when I'm already the kid with a dead mom and the same backpack since fifth grade?

Yeah. It matters.

It makes me a Neo-Maxi-Zoom-Dweebie.

"Want to hang out?" I ask Megan when we get to our street.

"Oh." She tips her head so her hair hides her face. Megan has the most perfect hair of all time. My mom called it honey blond. It's thick and shiny and cut so it's long on one side and short on the other. Not a frizzy, mousy-brown, shoulder-length mess like mine. The only thing dweebie about Megan is me. "Denny's coming over."

Her earlobe, on the exposed side, has two stud earrings through it. One is a real ruby chip her grandma gave her for her birthday last year. It's Megan's birthstone. The other is a gold heart. Everything about Megan is cooler than me.

Denny is her older brother. For the past six months, he's lived in an apartment with three of his friends. He's studying at CU

Denver, to be an engineer. Until the last couple of weeks, Denny coming home meant that Megan and I would be in their basement begging him to play one more game of foosball with us.

Not anymore. Apparently.

I smile like I'm not upset. Like I believe her. "I have homework anyway."

She stops when we get to her house. Her eyes move to my backpack, then up to my face. "I'll call after dinner."

I shift a little, trying to hide my milk carton from her. "All right."

I watch her walk away and wish that I could just throw the stupid thing into the trash can on the side of our house. After I grind it into the front lawn with the sole of my left Ked.

Except when I think about doing that, I think about the face of the kid that's printed on the back of the carton. A boy today. His name is Christopher Thorpe.

He's been living inside my brain since just after fourth period, when I took a milk carton from the big silver cooler in the cafeteria. I can't imagine ruining his face with my sneaker.

I swear, I used to be solidly normal. Not popular, but I blended in. I was just like Megan. Or at least a slightly less cool version of her.

I was just like pretty much everyone.

It isn't that my best friend is moving away from me. She's staying where we've always been, and I'm the one who's changing.

Yeah. Just call me Half-Orphan Girl with the Milk Cartons. Unfortunately, the title does not come with any superpowers. Just a rotating selection of "missing and exploited" sidekicks.

In my house, I turn on the kitchen faucet. While the water warms up, I carefully open the carton's top seam, then use a steak knife from the wooden block on the counter to cut out the bottom and the top flaps and slice open one side so I have a flat rectangle of waxed cardboard.

First a rinse to get rid of the milk residue that's gone a little sour. I never clean them at school. Not since Hillary MacLean caught me that one time in the bathroom by the gym.

She still calls me Cinderella, trying to make it stick. It hasn't, so far, but I'm not going to give her any more glue.

After the rinse, I squirt one drop of green dish soap onto the wet carton. Mom used it because of the commercials with the lady who says it's good for her hands.

Mom had nurse hands, dried out from being washed so many times every day. I can still feel their rough texture against my skin, if I close my eyes. The way her fingertips would catch in my hair as she brushed it off my forehead when she came in to turn out my light at night.

Sometimes we'd sit together at the kitchen table and soak our nails in little bowls of soapy green water, just like in the commercials.

Dad has not stopped buying Mom's soap. Using it to clean my milk cartons is a little like sharing my mom with these lost kids and that makes me feel a little bit like a hero. Like she was.

Mom was an army nurse during the Vietnam War. Before I

was born. She worked at the VA hospital, until she got sick, helping soldiers learn to walk again after they'd been injured.

When the carton squeaks under my fingers, it's clean enough. I'm careful not to soak the cardboard too much. It's a balance between sanitized and falling apart. I carefully pat it as dry as I can with a paper towel.

In my bedroom, inside the ballerina jewelry box that Aunt Louisa gave me when I turned six, there's a pair of scissors.

They're small and sharp, shaped like a golden bird with a long neck. Mom used them to snip threads when she sewed. I use them to carefully trim around the picture on the back of the milk carton.

When I push my finger and thumb into the holes to work the scissors, I imagine how often my mom's fingers were there. It's almost like we're holding hands. For a minute, I miss her a little less.

I collect a different picture most school days. That's important. There are no repeats. A boy. A girl. Brown hair, blond, red, black. One kid is bald. I think he might have cancer. Blue eyes, brown, hazel, green. White skin. Black. Brown. Freckled. Babies. Toddlers. Little kids. Kids my age. Teenagers. Some snapshots. A lot of school pictures.

Today's picture is a school portrait of a kid who is twelve, like me. A little alligator perches on the left side of his polo shirt and his wavy brown hair is long enough to brush the collar.

He looks like some of the boys in my class.

While I trim, I say his name exactly three times.

Christopher Thorpe.

Christopher Thorpe.

Christopher Thorpe.

I wonder if his friends call him Chris.

Then I say his birthday. He's only two weeks older than I am. He's probably finishing up sixth grade like I am.

And the place where he lives. *Cincinnati, Ohio.*

And the color of his hair and eyes. *Brown and brown.*

And his height and weight. *Five four, 130 pounds.*

I don't memorize his stats. Not yet. But I will. Eventually, I will. For now, my ritual is over, and I exhale as I pull a shoebox from under my bed and add Christopher Thorpe to my collection, alphabetically.

He is number thirty-nine and goes between Allora Simmons and Lisa Turner. And I say out loud, "You are the last one."

I've said that to myself for the last eight school days, and also when I added Juanito Diaz from our quart of milk at home over the weekend. So far, it hasn't worked. Maybe today it will.

At least now I can pull out my notebook and start on math homework. I've been thinking about Christopher Thorpe since 12:38 p.m., when I chose him after turning over four cartons. It's been worse. There are days I spend long, horrible minutes, turning every carton until I reach the last one and I'm sure there isn't a kid in the case that I don't already have.

Making sure there isn't a new kid is the only way I can skip carrying a milk carton around in my backpack all day. So, either way, I've gone from perfectly normal to that kid with the milk cartons.

The night before last I was up past midnight staring at the

ceiling with my heart pounding. There was no new kid that day. At least not in the milk cooler. It occurred to me for the first time that someone else might have had a boy or girl on their milk carton that I didn't have in my collection.

What if I'd missed a new kid because I took too much time getting into the cafeteria?

Today, I'd hurried in as fast as I could, pushing my way to the front of the line. And now I'm afraid that the next time I don't find a new kid in the cooler, I'll have to go look at the cartons sitting on tables. Or dig through the trash.

So now I'm that kid who insists on being first in line, turns over all the milk cartons in the cooler, and then carries her garbage—or maybe yours—home with her.

Fantastic. Thanks a lot, brain. It's not like I needed any help in the not-normal department.

I've stood in the cafeteria turning over milk cartons until kids notice. Until the lunch lady says *Just take one, they're all the same.* Until the school counselor calls me out of fifth period to talk to me about grief and healing. Until my dad says something vague about therapy.

It's a relief for Christopher Thorpe to let go of my brain.

✳ ✳ ✳

My dad's not big on rules. He never has been. That was always Mom's thing. But there's one he sticks to like glue. *No answering the phone during dinner.*

Even if dinner is just pizza, again.

Megan doesn't usually call during dinner, because she knows

she'll get the answering machine. But tonight, we're eating late. Also, again.

Dad's a high school history teacher, and for my whole life, he was home by 4:30 every day. But lately it's been more like six or seven. Even eight, like tonight, with a pizza or some Kentucky Fried Chicken.

So when the phone rings at a quarter after eight, we're still sitting at the kitchen table with a Pizza Hut box between us. He's telling me a story about how a kid in his second-period American History class tried to get him to raise his grade.

"Offered to do anything for extra credit," Dad says as the phone rings a second time. He draws his fingertips over his cheekbones. "Crocodile tears and everything. If they were real, I almost feel sorry for him."

"Are you going to give him extra credit?"

Dad lifts his eyebrows. "Maybe I should have him come clean your room. It would be like an archeological dig."

The answering machine picks up the call, and I hear Megan's voice. "Hey, Tessa. Um . . . guess you're still eating. Want to come over after? Call me back."

I look up at Dad. He takes another bite of his pizza, then says, "Go on."

"Are you sure?" Part of me wants him to make me wait until we're done eating. He was in the middle of a story, and I want things to be the way they used to be. I want him to stick to his one rule.

"I have papers to grade," he says. When I walk past him with my plate, he puts a hand on my arm to stop me. "Is your homework done?"

"Yeah."

He nods and goes back to his pizza, and I see him slipping away to wherever it is he goes when he's with me but not really with me. That's been happening even more than usual the last few weeks. Since Mrs. Benson, the school counselor, called him about the milk cartons.

"She needs time," he'd told Mrs. Benson. "Her mother just died. If some kids have to wait for a few minutes for their milk, I don't think it's the end of the world."

Mrs. Benson must have said something about that not being the point, but before he hung up, Dad said, "The point is that Tessa needs time, and I don't think it's asking too much to give her that. If I think she needs to talk to someone, I'll take care of that."

I go out the kitchen door into our backyard and through the hole in the oleander bush that I always use to get to Megan's house.

She must have heard me coming, because she opens her kitchen door before I can knock. "Denny's still here."

I smile. "We're so going to cream him this time."

It would be the first time, but she nods like it's a no-brainer. "Come on."

Our basement is full of dirt and spiders and the furnace. Megan's was turned into a rec room before they moved in. The walls and floors have paint and carpet instead of concrete and exposed pipes.

There's a little bar down there with a fridge that Megan's mom keeps full of Cokes. Megan opens it and gives me one, then takes one for herself.

Denny's standing at the foosball table with one of his dad's beers. He has dark-blond hair, like Megan. When he was in high school, he wore it short, but he's let the back grow out since he started college. He's trying to grow a beard, too, but it's not really working. Right now, he has a look on his face like he's been waiting hours for us to play him, two on one. "Ready to get your butts kicked?"

"Not this time," Megan says. "We're totally going to win."

We take our places. Megan and I on the left side of the table, Denny on the right. I'm in control of our defense, including the goalkeeper, and Megan takes the offense. We've been doing this a long time, and we don't have to talk about it.

I save, she scores, always.

Denny drops the ball, and the game starts. He can still beat us, even both of us together, but we're getting better. We've started to win sometimes.

And they're real wins, too. Denny never goes easy on us.

He slams the ball past my defense. I grunt as I reach to block with my keeper. Not quite fast enough this time. The ball goes in.

"Not bad, Tesseract." Denny's nickname for me is an inside joke. He's the only person who can get away with calling his sister Meg, and he's Denny—short for Dennis, which is close enough to Dennys—like the brother and sister from *A Wrinkle in Time*. And he always calls me Tesseract. "You almost had it."

"I'll get it next time." I take the ball out of the pocket.

He swallows the rest of his beer and shoots the can at the Broncos trash bin by the bar. It goes in, all net.

"Aren't we playing again?" I ask.

"Not tonight. I have a paper due Monday."

"Only one game?" I look at Megan, expecting her to help me convince her brother to stay longer. "I just got here."

Megan shakes her head, only she's not looking at me. She's looking at Denny. "It's okay. We can play again later."

"Plus, I've been here all afternoon," Denny says to me. "You should have come over earlier."

Right. A cold knot forms in the pit of my stomach. "It's okay."

"'Cause that other girl—"

Megan still doesn't look at me.

"Kind of sucks."

"What other girl?" I try to sound casual. Like my heart isn't beating hard. Like I don't feel a little sick.

Denny looks at Megan, who closes her eyes. He says, "See you guys later."

After he walks up the basement stairs, Megan finally looks at me. "Want to play again?"

"Sure." I really want this to be no big deal. I don't want it to mean that Megan lied to me about not being able to hang out after school. Or that she doesn't want to be my friend anymore.

She pulls the ball out of the pocket and takes Denny's side.

I get control after the drop. I use one of my midfielders to shoot it back to my defense, then nudge it toward the edge of the field before rocketing it down the line.

We play without talking. Megan gets the first shot, and I take the next two points. We play to five and then stop, both of us breathing hard, leaning against the table.

"It was Hillary, okay?" she says. "I didn't invite her. She just showed up."

I wonder if she thinks it's kinder to lie to me. I know that Hillary MacLean did not *just show up* at Megan's house with a sudden urge to play foosball.

"I think she has a crush on Denny," Megan says when I don't respond.

Weak.

"I had homework anyway."

Even weaker.

✳ ✳ ✳

By some unwritten, unspoken rule, after that day in the basement, Megan starts having Hillary over after school. They do their homework, she says. Hillary is in the gifted-and-talented program, just like Megan.

I'm just a regular seventh grader. Not gifted or talented.

I go over after dinner, and we hang out for a while until it's time to go home to bed. Hillary and I never cross paths.

Dad seems distracted lately. That's stewing in the back of my mind. Something's going on, and I don't know what it is.

Normally, I'd talk about it with Megan and try to figure it out. Instead, I just pretend everything is A-OK. Nothing to see here, folks.

*   *   *

A few days later, after I cut out Darian Marshall, aka milk-carton-kid number forty-four, I start on my non-gifted-and-talented homework and wonder if Hillary is over at Megan's.

So far, I've resisted the urge to hide in the oleander to see if she shows up. I've also had good luck finding new lost kids to add to my collection, and somehow those two things have mixed up in my head. Like, if I spy on Megan and Hillary, I'll jinx my milk-carton magic.

I push the idea of spying out of my head and just start working on my history homework instead.

TWO

"Hey, Cookie."

I look up, still sitting cross-legged on my bed, although I'm lost in a book called *Flowers in the Attic* now. It's about two brothers and two sisters who are locked in an attic by their mother and grandmother after their father dies. It's gruesome, but I'm so caught up in the story that when Dad pulls me out of it, I blink and realize for the first time that it's really too dark to read.

"Hey, Dad."

He flips my bedroom light switch, and the overhead fixture pops on. He doesn't warn me about ruining my eyes, the way Mom would have. I don't have to hide the book, which I probably shouldn't be reading, because I know that he won't ask me about it. "Get your homework done?"

I nod. "I only had history and a little Spanish."

"No math?"

"I got it all done in class."

"Good."

"What time is it?"

"About eight thirty. I'm sorry I'm so late."

I stand and go to pick up the pink phone on my desk. There's a ring tone. It just didn't ring. I hang it up again. "It's okay."

"I thought you might be at Megan's."

I shrug. Like, hey, no big deal that my dad didn't show up for dinner and my best friend didn't call me tonight. "Why were you out so late, anyway?"

"I brought home . . ." His eyebrows come together in a sort of bushy V between his eyes. He always looks tired lately, but there is something else going on. *Something is wrong.*

The smell of cheese and tomato sauce and grease hits my nose and makes my stomach rumble. I start to walk toward my bedroom door, bringing my book with me. "Pizza?"

"Yes," he says. "But . . ."

I don't want to hear what he's going to say. "Can I go to the library after school tomorrow? I want the next book in this series."

"Sure, but, Tessa—"

Something is wrong. I want to ignore it, but there's a reason they call it an elephant in the room.

Who can ignore an elephant?

My heart hurts like that elephant has reached its trunk into my chest, past my ribs, and is squeezing it. I step back and the blood drains from my face.

I fainted once, when I was ten years old. I was making pancakes with Mom and all of a sudden, I felt just like I do now. The next thing I knew, I was lying on the floor, with a sore elbow, a knot on the back of my head, and a wave of nausea washing over me. I was still holding the pancake turner.

Do not faint. I force myself to take a breath.

He puts a hand on my arm and the squeezing in my chest is worse. My knees go weak. I can't breathe. My book falls to the floor, bounces off the carpet, and lands on my bare foot. I shake my head, denying whatever he's about to say before he can even say it. But I still ask, "What's wrong?"

Dad picks up my book and puts it in my hand again without looking at it. Mom would never have let me read *Flowers in the Attic*, and I suddenly feel guilty for liking it so much. I toss it on my bed.

"Nothing," Dad says. "Nothing's wrong, Tessa. Baby, breathe."

I believe him instantly, and the faint feeling fades. My dad's parents died when he was in high school. I'm half an orphan. Orphans don't lie to each other, that's *our* unspoken rule. Even when Mom was sick and everyone else tried to tell me it wasn't so bad, Dad never once lied to me.

The panic leaves as fast as it came, and there's a hollow place left behind. Like I'm a chocolate Easter bunny, empty in the middle. I inhale and fill the space with oxygen.

"Well," I say, a little awkward. "Did you get pepperoni?"

"No, not this time." When I try to walk out to the kitchen, he puts a hand on my arm again and stops me. "I brought someone home to meet you."

I keep my back to him and close my eyes. "Who?"

He inhales and exhales, then does it again, like he's blowing himself up. I think about the old-fashioned bellows my gran has by her fireplace. I think about the Wizard of Oz's hot-air balloon. And I wonder when we're ever going to stop feeling so empty.

Finally, he just says, "Lila."

Whoever *Lila* is, I decide immediately that she's not really anyone. Another teacher at Dad's school. A neighbor. A distant cousin.

She is definitely not a *woman*. My dad has not brought a *woman* home to meet me, the way that Shannon Hadley's dad introduced her and her brother to a *woman* he was dating last year.

No way.

No. Way.

"Who's Lila?" I finally ask, when Dad doesn't say anything more or let go of my arm. "Is she a teacher?"

"A volunteer at school." He squeezes, then lets me go. "A literacy volunteer. Just be nice. Please."

He leaves my room without looking back.

I kind of want to close my door, turn the lock, and pretend there isn't a woman on the other side of it that my dad wants to introduce me to.

A woman he thinks he needs to warn me to be nice to.

It would work. For a while, anyway.

But not forever.

* * *

Lila looks like she walked right off the cover of one of the *Seventeen* magazines I have stacked on my nightstand.

I've always been on the short side, like my mom, who was only five two. Lila is about six feet tall. Close to as tall as my dad, who is six three. She's slender and all angles, in a hot-pink jumpsuit and a pair of gladiator sandals with black leather straps that wrap up over her ankles.

Her hair is sun-streaked blond. It's perfectly crimped and pulled up in a ponytail on the right side of her head. She pushes a loose strand behind her ear when she sees me.

She does not belong in our living room, and not just because I don't want her there. She should be at college, I think. In a dorm. Or somewhere getting her picture taken for *Seventeen* magazine.

"Hi," Lila finally says when neither my dad nor I say anything.

"Um, hi." The word comes out automatically, but my jaw feels rusty. Like I've forgotten exactly how to make all the parts of my mouth move together to form words.

"Okay." Dad inhales through his nose. "Let's do this."

Lila shoots him a sharp look, and I want to sink into the ground. I don't want to "do this." I want to cover my ears and stomp my feet and make him stop.

It would work for a while.

But not forever.

"Gordy." There's a tone in her voice that sparks a warning bell in me. But I'm stuck on her calling him *Gordy*. No one calls him Gordy. His friends sometimes call him Gordo—left over from when he was a kid. But mostly, he's just Gordon.

Or Mr. Hart if you're a literacy volunteer at his school.

Dad doesn't lie to me. Whatever *this* is, it's going to come out. Anyway, before I can try to hold it off, he takes a deep breath and the whole truth comes out with his exhale. "Lila and I are getting married."

I was so sure that he was going to say that he and Lila were going on a date that it takes a minute for me to understand what actually came out of his mouth.

My rusty jaw swings open. Lila's perfectly freckled cheeks are flushed, and she gives me a look that says she's sorry.

"What?" I ask. She closes her eyes and shakes her head once. I turn away from her, back to Dad. "What did you say?"

His look begs me to help him. To not make this harder on him than it has to be. "Tessa."

Right. I'll make it really easy. "You can't get married."

His shoulders sag a little. "I know it's sudden."

"You can't get married!" Why am I the only one who knows this? I slow down and talk to him like he's a little kid who doesn't understand. "You are *already* married."

He fidgets with the band on his left ring finger. "Tessa."

"You can't marry her!" I swing back to look at Lila, one arm sweeping to encompass all six feet of her. "I don't even know her."

Lila says, "I should go."

"I'll call you." Dad doesn't look away from me, though.

The facts:

Lila is a literacy volunteer at the high school where Dad teaches American and World History to ninth and tenth graders.

She's twenty-three.

She's pregnant.

My dad made her pregnant.

"She's going to have a baby," he says. Again. He's looking at me like he might break into a talk that starts with *When a man and a woman really love each other.* "I know it's . . . well, it's bad timing is what it is."

"Bad timing? Dad."

I wonder if any other girl, ever in the history of the world, has had to have this particular talk with her father. I've seen enough after-school specials to know that it happens the other way around sometimes with girls who are a little older than I am—a teenager has to tell her dad that she's pregnant.

But this? This is ridiculous. I don't even know what to say, so he just keeps talking. "We need a fresh start. You're going to like Lila. She's a—"

"A fresh start?" I cannot process any more facts. I don't want to know what Lila is. "This is a *fresh start*?"

"We need . . . something."

"You think we need *this*?"

He opens his hands in front of him. "It's what we have."

"How could you be so *stupid*?"

He lets my rudeness slide. Since Mom died, he pretty much lets anything slide. "Lila's father is giving her a house for a wedding gift."

That makes me blink in surprise. The pressure in my chest lets up a little. It's weird but at least a little better. "So she's not going to live here."

"Tessa." It's his turn to speak slowly. "He's giving *us* a house. All of us."

"We don't need a house." It's like we're speaking different languages, carefully pronouncing each syllable in the hopes that the other person will get the gist. "We already have one."

"The house is in California." I hold up a hand, trying to stop whatever he's going to say next. "Please. Please, Tessa. She can't live here. We can't live here with her."

"I'm not moving to California." I have never heard that begging tone in my dad's voice before, and it scares me. "You can't make me."

"Yes, I can."

"I'll move in with Gran."

The look on his face makes my heart hurt again. With a single word, he proves me wrong about letting me get away with anything. "No."

I add to my mental list of facts. He's right. Lila can't live in our house. The idea of her sleeping in my mom's bedroom makes me feel like I might really be sick.

And I can't leave him to live with my grandmother. Or, I suppose I could try, but I won't. I don't want to leave my dad. That was an empty threat, although it was true when I said it.

Even though it has been ten months, three weeks, and six days, I still have a hard time remembering from minute to minute that Mom is dead. I don't let myself think "gone" or "passed away." She's dead.

She survived being a combat nurse in Vietnam, but she got sick one year, ten months, and twenty-three days ago, and 368 days later, she died of breast cancer.

She would not leave my dad, and neither will I.

"I don't want to move to California," I say.

"The house is right on the beach. And really close to Disneyland." As if he's giving me the ocean and Micky Mouse as consolation prizes. *Your mother is dead. Your father got a twenty-three-year-old literacy volunteer pregnant. But at least you get to go to the Happiest Place on Earth.*

"I don't care." I've only ever lived in our house. My best friend lives next door. I started middle school this year, and it was the first time I'd ever changed schools. I've never been the new kid before.

Mom dying turned me into a milk-carton-hoarding weirdo. I can't even imagine what moving to California with my dad and his pregnant . . . whatever she is . . . who I only just met, will do to me.

Mom used to say that my imagination is too big for my body.

I am afraid right now, sitting across from my dad and trying to understand all these facts, that maybe I'll crack apart into hundreds of pieces.

"Let's give it a year," he says. "Please, Tessa. A year. If you hate it, we'll come home."

"We" doesn't just mean him and me. It never will again. And in a year, it won't just mean him and me and Lila, either. We both know that.

THREE

"Let her stay with me." Gran is Mom's mother, and she lives alone in a condominium complex for people fifty-five and older. Mostly much older, like her. When Dad starts to say, again, that I can't stay with her, her mouth purses. "Just until the end of the school year, anyway."

"No." Just the one word, like when I threatened this exact thing. Dad leaves no room for argument, and that helps. He will not move to California with Lila and leave me behind. He doesn't bother to tell her again that we aren't even leaving until school lets out in a couple of weeks anyway.

"I don't know how you could do this," she says quietly. "How could you do this to Maggie?"

Dad stiffens. This is the first time Gran has brought up Mom, and it feels like she's crossed a line. My anger shifts from Dad to Gran as he takes my arm and steers me toward the front door. "We'll be late."

"That was mean to say, Gran," I call over my shoulder.

Gran stops Dad with a hand on his elbow. "I'm sorry, Gordon. I know you didn't . . . that you wouldn't . . ."

His hand hovers over hers. "I just need to get through today."

"I can't go," Gran says. "I just can't."

"I know." Dad finally gives her hand a squeeze. "It's okay."

Having Gran at his wedding to Lila would be sort of like having Mom there. I try to think of something to say to make everything better, but there isn't anything.

Gran hugs me tight and walks down our sidewalk to her ancient yellow station wagon. The back is full of flats of flowers and they make me smile, despite the fact that I still feel as hollow as a chocolate Easter bunny. No matter how crazy the world has gone, my gran will have flowers on her patio just like every summer.

"Ready?" Dad asks.

I'm not. I can't even imagine that I'll ever be ready for this. But when he opens the door to his blue Chevy pickup truck, I climb in.

I have added a few more facts to my list over the last couple of weeks, mostly from eavesdropping. Dad is glad that all of this is happening so close to summer. He is afraid that he would have lost his job, if they knew that the reason we're moving to California is because he's marrying Lila. And he's afraid that if he was fired, he would never get a job again.

The baby is due in August. I took my puppy calendar off the wall and counted back. Lila is approximately 198 days pregnant.

Dad has applied for a California teaching license, and he has an interview set up at a high school near the house Lila's father gave her.

He did that before he brought Lila home for dinner a couple

of months ago. It was already decided by the time I met her. I think Dad has probably known about the baby for a while.

They are getting married today, at the courthouse. Lila's family was invited, but they didn't come. Maybe they can't, like Gran can't. Maybe they're angry at my dad the way I imagine he'd be angry if I married a forty-year-old man when I'm twenty-three.

Or maybe they aren't here because Los Angeles is a thousand miles away.

I don't know the answer, but I'm curious.

Lila's waiting for us to pick her up. She hasn't been back to our house since that first time. Dad hasn't made me see her again. He asks every few days if I want to and I say no, and he lets me get away with it.

That's all about to stop.

When we pull up to her apartment complex, she's standing out front in a white cotton sundress. She is even more beautiful than I remembered.

And now that I know the facts, she is very obviously pregnant. She looks like she has a small planet tucked under her dress.

"She looks like California." I'm not sure where that came from or what I mean by it. It just comes out. Maybe it's about the way it looks like the sun has got caught in her long hair.

Dad doesn't respond. Instead he just looks at her and says, "We're going to be okay."

I'm not sure if he's trying to convince me or himself. It sounds like he believes it, though. He puts an arm around me and pulls me closer to him when Lila opens the passenger door. She climbs in beside me.

None of us talk on the way to the courthouse. That rusty feeling is back in my jaw, and I don't think I could speak, even if I had something to say.

They are married by a short, round woman with steel-gray hair that's permed as curly as steel wool. She tells a story about a rose and how it needs water and good soil to bloom, and then a few minutes later, she marries my dad to this person who is not my mother.

He puts a gold band on Lila's finger. I'm relieved that it doesn't look anything like Mom's wedding ring. It didn't occur to me that Dad might give Mom's wedding ring to Lila until that moment. In the next instant, I know that he never would have.

Lila has a similar gold band for my dad, and there is an awkward moment when she realizes that he's still wearing his original wedding ring.

"Oh," the woman marrying them says. "Well."

Dad closes his hand in a fist, instead of trying to take his wedding ring off. I expect Lila to be upset. I would be, if I were getting married and my future husband refused to take off his old wedding ring.

She surprises me, though.

She takes his right hand and slips the ring onto it, then turns back to the woman with her chin lifted, like she's daring the judge to judge her.

There are a few more things to say about not letting the sun go down on anger and what the State of Colorado has authorized her to do, and the woman ends with, "You may kiss your bride."

Dad does. Lila's fingers tighten in the back of his shirt. His tangle in her hair, long and loose like sunshine flowing down her back. The kiss only lasts a few seconds, and then they're married.

✳ ✳ ✳

"It won't be so bad," Megan says on the second-to-last day that I'll live in Denver. We're in her basement, probably for the last time ever. "I mean, Los Angeles. You'll probably see famous people."

I slam one of my foosball posts all the way toward her, blocking a shot, probably harder than I needed to. "I don't *care* about famous people."

She tries to fake me out, pretending to punt, but then sends the ball toward my goal. "But what if you see, like, movie stars?"

I block her again, easy as pie, and send the ball back to her keeper. "I'm not going to see movie stars, Megan."

My shot sinks.

"Dang it." She straightens up and spins her keeper in a slow, lazy circle. "Well, you might."

"You sound like you want me to go."

Mom would have called this *low-hanging fruit*. The easiest way to feel better is to get Megan to tell me that she wants me to stay. That she's going to miss me. Instead, Megan goes quiet while she fishes the ball out of the pocket on her side of the table. Too quiet for too long.

"You want me to go?" I ask.

"Not really."

What is that supposed to mean?

"It's just . . . maybe it will be good for you. And California sounds cool and all. I mean, it's a *beach* house."

Would it be good for *her* if *her* dad all of a sudden married some other woman? Some other *pregnant* woman? "I don't care about a beach house."

"Maybe you'll be able to stop . . ." I know what she's thinking. Maybe I'll be able to stop the milk-carton thing. And she doesn't say it, but I think she's thinking maybe without me and my milk cartons around, she can just be perfectly normal again. Maybe even better than normal.

Without me, she could be popular. I've probably been holding her back since kindergarten. "I need to finish packing."

She doesn't try to stop me when I leave.

❋　❋　❋

Megan watches from the end of her driveway as we pull away in Dad's pickup. The bed is packed with everything we're bringing with us to California.

I've cried so much, my eyes hurt. My head hurts. Everything hurts. I crane my neck to see through the side-view mirror until Megan and the For Sale sign stuck in our front lawn are out of sight.

Dad doesn't say anything. He's already apologized a thousand times. It hasn't changed the fact that we're driving away from home. Forever. Or that there is a giant SOLD! sticker across the front of the For Sale sign. Another family is moving into our house.

Some other girl gets to sleep in my bedroom, next door to Megan. She'll do her homework in the dining room where Mom used to help me with my math. She'll go to my school. Maybe she'll sit in my seats, use my textbooks. Be my best friend's new best friend.

Maybe Megan will eat lunch with the new girl. She'll hang out with Hillary MacLean more, I'm pretty sure. It makes me want to cry all over again to think about that.

"I'm sorry, Cookie," Dad says once we're out of our neighborhood. An apology. Again. He can't help himself. I know he really is sorry, but I wish he'd thought about how sorry he'd be before he got us into this mess.

Even *I* know what condoms are for.

Lila drove her own car back to California the day after the wedding. It's a purple convertible Karmann Ghia that looks like it came from the same Easter basket as the hollow chocolate bunny I sometimes feel like I'm turning into.

She went to get the new house ready. It's not new to her, though. She grew up in it, Dad told me. She gets to live in her childhood home, and I don't.

None of this is fair.

Dad looks at me, but before he can apologize again, I prop my feet on the dashboard. I put my headphones over my ears and I look out the window, at Denver, for the last time.

Dad tugs one earphone off my ear. "You'll be back here, Cookie. To visit Gran, at least."

"Whatever." I settle the music back where it belongs. But not before I hear Dad mutter, *This is going to be a long trip.*

He's right.

✳ ✳ ✳

Dad puts down his coffee and leans across the table toward me.

"Here's the thing," he says. We're at a McDonald's somewhere in Utah, eating Egg McMuffins before we start driving for the second day. I feel like I've been on this stupid road trip my whole entire life.

"What's the thing?" I ask when he doesn't actually tell me what the thing is.

"I need you to stop being mad at me."

Really? "Well, I need you to stop making me move to California to live with . . . with someone I don't even know."

"You will know her."

"I don't want to!"

"You have to." Dad takes a swallow of his coffee and then rubs his eyes under his glasses. "We're going to be a family, Tessa. You'll see."

"I thought we already were a family." Egg McMuffin turns to Bowling McBall in my stomach. "This isn't fair."

"Trust me," he says. "I know."

"I don't even know her." Déjà vu. We've been around this block before. Many times, especially in the last twenty-four hours.

He puts his coffee down. "That's my fault. Not hers."

"*She's* making us move to California," I point out.

"*She* isn't making us do anything." He shakes his head. "I couldn't—"

30

I've heard this before, too. "We could've moved to a different house in Denver. You could've not—"

He puts up a hand to stop me.

"This isn't fair," I say. We're both just repeating ourselves now.

"I wish I could make life fair for you, Tessa. I can't. I'm sorry, I can't."

It's on the tip of my tongue to scream *I hate you* right in the middle of a Utah McDonald's, but he looks so sad, the words dry up before I can. They aren't true anyway, and Dad and I don't lie to each other.

※ ※ ※

We spend the second day pretty much like the first, and the second night at a Motel 6 in Las Vegas. On the third day of our road trip, we arrive in California.

I'm nervous all of a sudden. I feel a million miles from home. Like we're moving to the moon, not just a few states west. "Why did Lila's parents give her a house?"

Dad drums his thumbs on the steering wheel a moment before he answers. "Because they could, I suppose."

"They're rich?"

He nods slowly. "I guess they are."

"Are they going to be there?" What I really want to know, but won't let myself ask, is *Are they going to like me?* Also, do they hate him?

"No." He turns away from the road for a second to look at me. "They're spending the summer in Jamaica."

There is something about what he says that I don't quite understand. Some catch in his voice. "Are they mad at her?"

"Not mad," he says.

I know the part that he doesn't say. I've heard it before, when I've done something wrong. They're not mad. They're disappointed.

We finally pull up in front of a tall, narrow white house that really is right on the beach.

The good thing about the drive from Denver to Los Angeles being so long is that I'm ready for it to be over now, no matter where we are.

Anyway, the beach smells good. Fresh and fishy at the same time. It's weird that's even possible, but it is. I can see the ocean, only a few shades deeper blue than the sky, and I want to walk to it. See it.

"Dad," I say. "Is that the beach?"

He looks toward it and nods. "Let's get unpacked."

The front door opens, and Lila comes out of it and down the walk. Dad hugs her, but she has to lean in, over her round belly.

She looks at me, but I turn all my attention to the house before she can say anything. I'm not sure what I'll do if she tries to hug me, too. I take a step away, just in case.

The house has three stories and is perfectly square. Like a tower, almost. The top floor has a wide balcony that goes all the way around it.

Lila sees me looking up at it and says, "That's your room. It was mine when I was a kid. It always made me feel like a princess."

I look from her to my dad. I've landed in some bizarre world where I'm about to start living in the bedroom that his wife, who is one hundred percent not my mother, was probably still sleeping in five years ago.

"At least we won't lock you in," he says. Lila and I both gape at him. He blinks and, for a second, looks as confused as I feel. "Like the kids in your book."

My eyebrows shoot up. "You read *Flowers in the Attic*?"

He shrugs a shoulder. "Mom always read everything you did."

Mom's not here. I cannot make those words come past my rusty jaw.

"Let me show you the room," Lila says. "You're going to love it here."

I shift my backpack and hear Mom's voice in my ear saying, *Be brave, Tessa.* My mother was a hero. She saved soldiers' lives before I was born, and she would not like to see me standing in front of a beach house bawling about something I can't change.

Dad puts an arm around me, and we go in together.

✳ ✳ ✳

The house is tall, but it isn't very big. The ground floor consists of a living room and kitchen and bathroom. No dining room, just a small table and chairs next to a sliding-glass door that leads from the kitchen to a patio in the backyard.

The second floor is Lila's bedroom and another bathroom. I know that it's really Lila and Dad's bedroom, but I can't go there yet.

The third story of the house that Lila's parents gave her as a wedding present is just one room—like a cherry perched on top of a cupcake. Lila called it mine, but I stand in the doorway and know that she's lied to me.

This is not my bedroom.

"You're having a girl?" I ask her.

She looks around the room and smiles. "I think so."

While Dad and I were finishing the school year and packing up the only home I've ever lived in, Lila was busy turning her old bedroom into a nursery.

It's painted pink. The exact shade of the Canada mints my gran likes. They taste like stomachache medicine to me. In fact, this whole room looks like one giant stomachache.

Wallpaper lines the bottom half of the room on all four sides. It's printed with brightly colored girl dolls holding hands. The top half of every wall has big windows and there's a sliding-glass door. It's like being inside a doll's lighthouse.

There's a crib with lacy bedding against one wall and billowy white curtains on all of the windows.

The pink paint and doll paper haven't been put there for me. But there's a twin bed against one wall with a headboard that has built-in cubbies with sliding doors. It's made with a fluffy white comforter and two sky-blue pillows. Lila took the door off the closet and there's a desk inside. A bulletin board hangs on the wall in front of it.

She's cut my name out of glittery paper and tacked the letters to the board.

There's a stack of *Seventeen* and *Tiger Beat* magazines sitting on top of the desk. Dad must have told her I like them. But it's what's sitting on the bed that makes me come deeper into the room for a closer look.

Petals on the Wind. The next book, after *Flowers in the Attic.* I never got it from the library. In fact, I've barely read anything since the day I met Lila.

"Do you like it?" she asks.

I turn to look at her. "It's so pink."

She beams, like I've complimented her. "I always wanted to paint it pink. My mother likes neutrals."

I look at the candy-pink walls again. Before I can think of anything to say, Lila turns and leaves me alone in the room.

My shoebox fits perfectly in one of the cubbies at the head of the bed, behind the sliding door. My ballerina jewelry box, with my mother's little scissors, will go on top when I unpack it.

I feel a little weird sitting on the bed. It's not mine. We didn't bring any furniture. My bed is sitting in a storage unit in Denver.

I wonder if Lila slept in this bed growing up.

Homesickness hits me like a sucker punch. I don't want to be here. I can't believe that I have to live in California, in this house, with Lila and a baby.

"Tessa!" Dad's voice carries up two flights of stairs like it's nothing. *Acoustics*, I think, and the word popping up in my head helps me pull myself together. My choir teacher from the fifth grade taught us about acoustics. This is an old house, and sounds carry up the stairs like they're a highway for words.

When I come down the two flights, Dad and Lila are in the kitchen. Lila is putting away the leftover road-trip snacks. Dad is staring at the open pantry like maybe she's keeping a skeleton in that closet.

"Are we unloading now?" I follow Dad's gaze and stop like I've run into a brick wall. "Whoa."

There are at least fifty boxes of trash bags in the pantry. The big black kind my dad puts leaves in when he rakes the yard. And toothpaste. Dozens of red boxes of cinnamon toothpaste. Each one with a toothbrush attached to it.

There are also gallon jars of peanut butter and mayonnaise. More than we could eat in a year.

I look up at my dad and open my mouth. I'm not sure what I'm going to say, but it doesn't matter. Dad shakes his head once to stop me and says, "Let's get the truck unpacked."

Lila comes to help, even though she's so pregnant now that she waddles when she walks.

"You'll have to share a bedroom with the baby." *Yeah. The crib and doll wallpaper gave that away.* How I feel about that must show on my face, because she hurries to add, "But not for a while. A few months at least. I got a great deal on a bassinet that we can keep in our room until she outgrows it."

Our room makes my heart skip a beat.

I want to ask how she knows the baby will be a girl, but it's like my brain can't figure out this whole stringing-words-together thing.

Lila doesn't seem to notice. She picks up a suitcase and just keeps chattering. "I'm so glad you guys are finally here. I was thinking that we should go to Disneyland before the baby is born.

Who knows when we'll be able to go if we wait. Have you ever been to Disneyland?"

"No," I say. "I haven't."

I shoot Dad a look. He says, "Let me carry that."

"Oh, it's not heavy." Lila carries the suitcase toward the house.

Dad stands, watching her go, then shakes himself. "Okay, Cookie. Let's do this, huh?"

We didn't actually bring much. Before we left Denver, we had a garage sale and moved the rest of our house, including all of Mom's things, into storage.

A few nights before we left, I'd laid awake in my bed and eavesdropped on Dad's half of a phone call with Lila.

We're just bringing clothes and books and things.

No. No dishes.

Lila, I'm definitely not bringing my bed. Just what we can fit in the truck. Everything else is going in storage.

I know what it costs. I rented the unit.

Honey, I don't care if we eat off paper plates for the rest of our lives. We'll be there at the end of the week. I just want to get there.

He calls her Honey. I've heard it on other phone calls, when he doesn't know I'm listening. The truth is that I don't care. For all of my life, he's only ever used two other pet names.

I'm Cookie. My mom is Cream. It started when she was pregnant with me. He can call Lila anything he wants, as long as it isn't Cream. Or Cookie, I suppose. But especially not Cream.

Dad lifts my bike out of the truck bed. The front tire has gone flat.

"We'll fix that tomorrow."

"Should I put it in the garage?"

Dad looks toward the garage that he's seeing for the first time, same as me. "I think so."

"Wait!" Lila says at the same time. When we turn to look at her, she bites at her bottom lip. "It's okay. We'll make some room."

The pantry was weird. The garage, though. Wow. Lila removes a huge padlock, and when Dad lifts the door over his head, I don't even know what to say. Or think.

There is a wall of disposable diapers on one side. Dozens of packages in all sizes. And another wall of paper towels along the back. And another of toilet paper on the other side. And in the middle, filling the whole garage, there are industrial-looking metal shelves lined with cold cereal and baby food and boxes of macaroni and cheese. I see mouthwash and a whole row of shampoo.

It's like some kind of grocery store. In a garage. There is nowhere for my bike. Or any of the things I kept in the garage at home. My pop-up soccer goal. My sled. My skis. Or Dad's tools. Or Mom's box of nursing textbooks.

I wonder if this is why we left it all in storage in Denver.

"Here." Lila uses her hip to shove a stack of cases of applesauce farther down a row between two shelving units. "You can park it here."

I look at Dad and he nods, so I wheel my bike in.

"For now," Lila says.

We're on our way back to the house when Dad lifts the top off a big green garbage bin. His paper coffee cup bounces off a half-gallon milk container and falls into the can.

I'm frozen in my tracks, like the concrete under my feet has turned to goo that's got my sneakers stuck tight.

"So, I'm thinking pizza for dinner," he says. Dad could eat fast food for every meal. Mom said he has the palate of a ten-year-old.

Lila makes a sad little whining noise. "But I bought stuff to make fish tacos for your first night."

I want to say that Dad doesn't like fish. Or spicy food. But I can't. I'm still back at the trash can. And the milk carton.

Don't do it, Tessa. I take a breath. *You don't need to look at that carton.*

Half-gallon milk cartons have bigger pictures on the back than the pints at school, with two kids instead of one.

Two missing kids.

Lost. Kidnapped. Stolen. Run away. Wandered off.

Two kids that I cannot bring myself to leave in Lila's trash can if I don't already have them in my shoebox.

I take the lid off the can, even as my brain screams at me to stop this right now. *Right this minute, young lady.*

Do not pull garbage out of Lila's can.

Don't do it.

I have a moment of hope that the carton will have kids on it that are already in my collection. That lasts as long as it takes me to flick a banana peel away and turn the waxed cardboard over.

I'm going to have to carry the carton inside with me. And wash it in front of Dad and Lila. I have a bottle of green dish soap in my backpack, which is still in the third-floor bedroom.

Lila's nose wrinkles when she sees me, and even that's pretty. "What're you doing?"

39

I look at the kitchen sink. There's a bottle of orange dish soap sitting behind the faucet. I test out the idea of using it on my milk carton, but I know right away that I can't.

I can't.

"Come on, Tessa," Dad says quietly. "You don't have to do this anymore."

Why did I leave my backpack up there? "I'll be right back."

"Tessa."

I take the carton with me up the stairs. I'm aiming for casual. Like fishing old milk cartons out of the trash and carrying them around the house is *no big deal*. Nothing to see here, folks.

I hear Lila whisper, her voice carrying up the acoustic stairs after me. "What is she doing, Gordy?"

Dad shushes her as I hit the first landing.

"But she can't take garbage up to the baby's room."

At least the truth about whose room it really is, is out. Dad says something I can't make out as I open the bedroom door on the third floor.

I'd put a plastic sandwich bag over the top of my soap bottle before we left Denver and held it in place with a hair tie. I had a vague idea that I might find myself with a milk carton on the road. I didn't. But I'm glad I'm not going to have to try to get Dad to take me to the market tonight to pick up the right brand.

"You really have lost it," I say as I take the soap out of my backpack. "You know that, right? You really have."

The only sink between me and the kitchen is in the bathroom on the second floor. The bathroom next to Lila's bedroom.

I still can't make myself even think *Lila and Dad's bedroom.* And I can't go in there.

I go down the second flight of stairs to the ground floor. Dad and Lila are on the back patio. Sound carries around the house like magic, but I can't hear them talking at all through the sliding-glass door.

Dad's dumping charcoal into a small black grill. No pizza, then. I start to go to the sink, to get my ritual over with before they come back in, but I stop when I see that there are bags of charcoal stacked against the patio wall. Lots of bags.

Dad looks up at me as Lila takes the empty bag from him, puts it on the ground, and wraps her arms around his neck.

Except for the kiss at their wedding and the hug when we arrived, I've never seen Dad and Lila touch. I look away now and turn on the faucet. My heart thuds in my chest as I carefully open the milk carton's seams.

Rinse in warm water. Add a single drop of soap. Then two more, because this carton is way bigger than the pints I bring home from school. Also, it stinks way worse. The scent of the soap filters up and smells like my mom.

My fingers feel weird, like they're not quite attached to my hands. I keep my face turned away from the sliding-glass door, because I can't let myself see Dad with Lila when the kitchen smells like Mom.

When the carton is clean, I pat it dry and carry it back upstairs. I pull my ballerina jewelry box from the suitcase Dad carried up earlier, and I sit cross-legged on the bed.

Use Mom's crane scissors to cut the two kids from the back of the carton.

Whisper their stats.

File them away alphabetically.

"These are the last ones. I can't do this anymore."

"Tessa?"

I jump when Dad's voice filters not up the stairs or through the door, but from the floor. Through a heater vent nearly under the bed.

"Yeah?" I say back.

"Dinner in fifteen."

He's in the bedroom beneath mine. It's not just Lila's room. It's his, too.

"Tessa?" His voice is sharper, demanding that I answer.

"Okay."

✳ ✳ ✳

Dad does a good job of pretending he likes the fish tacos, even though for as long as I've been alive, he hasn't willingly put fish into his mouth.

I think they actually taste pretty good.

"We could take a walk down to the beach after dinner," Lila says.

"Sure." Dad starts to clear the table. All it takes is turning around and setting them on the sink just behind him.

Lila looks at me. I realize that she's waiting for me to respond to the beach idea. "Sure," I say.

"Great." She pulls herself out of her chair with a little noise, her hand sliding over her lower back like it's aching.

"We can do these dishes," Dad says, then looks at me.

I stand up and move to help, but Lila waves us away. "Don't be silly. You've been driving for days. I've got this. It's good for me to move around anyway."

She starts water running and pushes a black plug into the drain to let the sink fill.

And then she picks up the bottle of green soap that I left on the counter earlier.

My breath catches, but before I can say anything, she squirts a stream of my soap—of my mother's soap—under the running water.

The smell fills the kitchen immediately. It overpowers the fish. It overpowers me. It smells like Mom. It smells like Denver. It smells like my house. I grab the bottle off the counter. "That's mine."

"Oh." Lila takes a step back from me.

"That's mine!" Louder this time. "You can't use it."

"Tessa." Dad puts a hand out for me, but I duck away from him.

Can't he smell her? Tears fall down my cheeks. I expect Dad to reach for me again, to open his arms and invite me in to make everything okay. Instead, he turns to Lila, who is staring at me with wide blue eyes, the way she might stare at a raccoon that's wandered into her kitchen. A little disbelief. Some fear.

Dad shakes his head and says, "I'm sorry, Lila. I don't know what's gotten into her."

I take the soap with me and run up both flights of stairs.

FOUR

There isn't a lock on the bedroom door. I close it and then take my shoebox out of the cubby in the headboard and wedge myself into a spot on the floor between the foot of the bed and the closet.

The box smells faintly of sour milk and dish soap. It's almost pleasant, but not quite. I take the lid off and flip through the cards, saying the kids' names in order.

Christine Adams

Craig Alphonse

Richard Carlson

Elizabeth Dixon

There is something wrong with me. No one should get this upset about dish soap. No one.

I get all the way to *Erin Worth* and then look at the bedroom door. I don't hear Dad's footsteps. I don't hear any voices.

He's not coming to check on me.

He's probably busy making sure Lila is okay.

I start with *Christine Adams* again. With each name, my heart slows. With each name, the angry energy drains from me. I lean against the end of the bed, my fingers brushing over the cards.

* * *

I must have fallen asleep, because the next thing I know, it's nearly dark and my box has tipped over. The missing-kid cards are in a pile between my legs.

I have no idea where I am for the first couple of breaths. It's like waking up inside a dream. I stand up and move away from the mess, so I don't step on any of the kids.

"Dad?" It comes back to me slowly, starting when I see the baby's crib. I am not at home. "Daddy?"

"We're going to figure this out."

I turn, still disoriented. Dad's voice came from behind me, but he's not there.

"It's the first day. Give her time."

I sink to my knees and move closer to the vent on the floor near the bed. While I'm down there, I start to pick up the spilled cards, automatically putting them back in order. Christine Adams. Craig Alphonse. Richard Carlson. Elizabeth Dixon.

Dad's in the bedroom below mine with Lila. I hear her voice, but it doesn't carry as well as his does. When I have my milk-carton kids safely back where they belong, I crawl closer to the vent and bend nearer to it.

"It was dish soap," Lila says. "She completely freaked out over dish soap."

"The kind her mother uses."

"Used."

"What?"

"The kind Maggie used."

There's silence, and I wonder if Dad's heart aches the way mine does right now. "Right," he finally says. "Right."

Their voices lower, and even when I put my ear right on the vent, I can't make out what they're saying. Or not all of it. Just words that break through.

✳ ✳ ✳

She says, "I missed you."

And then the tone changes. It takes a minute for me to realize what's going on down there, and when I do, I sit up fast enough to bang into the bed behind me.

I cover my ears with my hands and take a ragged breath.

No. No. No.

I stand up and back away from the vent, hugging my box to my chest. I can't be here. I can't be in this house right now. I look around the room, panic building like a wall around me.

The only way down is past their bedroom and I can't. I really, really can't.

There's a sliding-glass door in the wall across from my bed. I pull it open and inhale deeply when cool ocean air hits me in the face.

The balcony is about six feet wide. I shut the bedroom door and walk to the wall. It's waist-high, and I bend over it, inhaling deeply.

When I can breathe again, I walk to one corner, looking for a chair. There isn't one, so I walk to the next. No chair, but there's the top of a staircase that leads all the way down to the lawn.

I'm gone before I even really decide to go, scrambling down

the stairs and then running across the lawn to the sidewalk. I bring my box with me, because I don't really have a choice.

I hope that carrying it around doesn't become a thing. I really can't handle any more *things*.

The house behind Lila's is ginormous and looks haunted to me. It's old and covered in ivy and windows with a thousand little panes.

Across the street from that house is a grass bluff. Below it is the Pacific Ocean. It is spectacular. Gentle waves lap at the clean brown sand, and just seeing it makes the fist that's clenched inside my chest let go.

I stand there watching a giant ship on the horizon, all lit up like a Christmas tree. No crashing waves, like in the movies. Just a soft movement that makes me want to walk into it.

The sun is sinking into the ocean, all orange and yellow, and most everyone has already gone home.

I should go back, because when my dad realizes that I left he's going to be pretty angry. At least, I think he is. Maybe he'll let it go, since I'm Half-Orphan Girl and he just made me move to California.

But first I want to get closer to the shore. Just for a minute. I want to feel the sand and the water. There's a wide wooden staircase a few yards to my left.

I'm nearly to the bottom, walking carefully in my bare feet, when a family passes me. The mom's got a giant red umbrella over her shoulder, and the dad's lugging a blue-and-white cooler. There are four little kids behind them, and they're all as pink as my new bedroom walls. They must have been here all day.

I push against the railing, then slide around it out of the way when I reach the bottom. One of the kids stumbles, and the mom swings around, nearly taking me out with her umbrella.

"Come on, Lindsey," she says. "Be careful."

If she hadn't nearly knocked me over, I would never have noticed the backside of the staircase.

The bluff is hollowed out back there, almost like a shallow, wide-mouthed cave. I forget about the family and take a step farther into the space. I have to squint to see in the dusk, but there are plastic milk crates in a half circle around a tipped-over old grocery cart that someone's been burning wood in.

There's a cooler, similar to the one the dad just hauled up the stairs. Only this one is propped open and the inside is filled with stuff.

I take another step closer to see, going all the way in. Comic books. Empty soda bottles. A canteen. A bag of marshmallows, closed with a wooden clothespin. A bunch of pulled-open wire hangers with the sticky black remnants of burned sugar on the tips.

"This is a clubhouse," I say.

"Yeah, it is."

I turn on the ball of one foot toward the voice. Unfortunately, the ball of that foot had landed on a rock or something because pain shoots up my leg and my knee crumbles.

I have time to see a boy silhouetted against the clubhouse's opening before I fall. He reaches for my arm and keeps me on my feet. "God, I'm sorry. Are you okay?"

"I think so." I hold on tighter to my box.

The boy tilts his head. "I haven't seen you around here before."

"Um, yeah," I say. "I'm new."

He's tall. At least six inches taller than I am. He's lanky to the point of being skinny, but he fills the clubhouse. I think he's about my age.

His skin is golden, and he has a head full of black hair that sticks up around his head in a tangle of wild curls. His eyes should be brown, but they aren't. Even without a lot of light, I can see that one is a green. The other is bright blue.

And they are both focused on my box of lost kids.

I suddenly feel like I've been caught trespassing. Like I've wandered into a stranger's house without being invited.

"What's your name?" he asks.

I take a breath and make myself say, "Tessa."

"Tessa." He says my name slowly, and my cheeks burn.

"Theresa." I have to say something or else I'm going to have to tunnel into the sand under my feet. "It came out Tessa when I was a baby. Just stuck, I guess."

"Tessa," he says one more time. Then he points at my box.

Before he can say anything else, I ask, "What's yours?"

"Jay Jay." Jason, I wonder. Or James. Or Jacob. Or John. He must be able to read my mind because he says, "Joshua. Junior."

"Junior."

"Yeah. Well, I think my grandma didn't want to have to yell my dad's name at me every time I piss her off. So I've always just been Jay Jay."

And just like that, balance is restored. I can breathe again. "You piss her off a lot?"

He tilts his head from side to side, and his face cracks into a wide smile. "It's how we do, you know?"

I shift my bare feet in the sand. "You live with your grandma?"

"Yeah." He points over my shoulder. "Big house on the corner."

My eyes go wide, and I look that way, like I might be able to see right through the wall of the clubhouse, up over the bluff and across the street, to the house he must be talking about. The house just in front of the one Lila grew up in. "The Haunted Mansion."

"It's not haunted," he says. "But yeah. That one."

"My dad and I just moved in behind you."

"Oh yeah?" He sounds truly surprised.

"Um. Yeah."

"So what are you doing down here?" he asks, changing the subject. Maybe hoping I won't ask why his grandma doesn't want to call him by his father's name. Or why he lives with her and not his parents. Sharing something to balance things is one thing. Having to *discuss* it is something totally different. Not that I would ask anyway. I've only known him for a couple of minutes.

So I say, "I don't know. Nothing."

He looks at the box again, and my face is burning so hard I'm afraid it might spontaneously combust.

"What's in your box?" he asks. Not mean or threatening, just curious. I put it behind me, both hands holding it against the small of my back. Like maybe out of sight will be out of mind.

Only, no such luck. He says, "Comic books? Cigarettes?"

"What?" I stumble back a step. "No."

He laughs and fakes right, then tries to reach around me to the left. "Oh my God. Do you have a *joint* in there?"

"No, I don't have a . . ." I try to sidestep him, and I rap my shin on the edge of the shopping cart firepit. My box falls, and the cards inside flitter to the ground like wingless birds.

The tears I've been holding back since—oh, somewhere in Nevada—fall down my face as I sink to my knees. Some of the little squares of waxed cardboard fall into the ashes of the firepit. I reach in, as carefully as I can.

"Oh man," Jay Jay says under his breath. "I'm sorry."

He kneels beside me and starts to pick up my cards from the sand. They're bright white, so even in the failing light, they shine.

"Fifty-two," I say, even though I know I sound like a crazy person. "I have fifty-two."

"Fifty-two what?" he asks, holding one of the cards up. "What are these?"

I pull the card from his fingers and put it in my box. "Never mind."

"But seriously." He picks up another one and brushes sand from it. "What are they?"

"Kids, okay?" I take that one, too. "They're missing kids."

Jay Jay picks up a third card and holds it close to his nose, then pulls it away sharply. "Like from milk cartons."

"Yes, exactly like from milk cartons." *Fine. Just fine.* I didn't want any friends in California anyway. I pull a card from the firepit and rub it against my T-shirt. "So, what even is this place?"

"A clubhouse, I guess, like you said." He adds a few more cards to the box. "So is that fifty-two?"

I can't see him well enough now to know if he's making fun of me. I also can't leave this clubhouse without all fifty-two of my cards, so I sit on the sand and start to count them.

He stands across from me, watching with his strange eyes.

Fifty-one. I count again, to be sure, then set the box aside and peer into the shopping cart firepit again. Jay Jay gets on his hands and knees in the sand and starts to feel around. "How many are you missing?"

"One." I won't know which one until I get home and put them back in order. If I can make myself leave this cave without all of my cards. *Come on. Come on, please, where are you?*

I don't realize that I'm crying until Jay Jay says, "Even if we don't find it tonight, we can look in the morning. It'll be okay."

His voice is soft and slow, like he's trying to calm a scared animal.

I want to stand up and brush off my knees and say, *Great, thanks.* Instead, I reach my hand down into the firepit and sift through the ashes.

Right now, this is about as embarrassing as turning over every milk carton in the cooler at school. In about sixty seconds, it's going to turn into the most embarrassing thing ever. He's going to have to go get my dad. I can feel it, churning in the pit of my stomach. This is the moment that will define my California experience, and it won't be good.

I am going to be a friendless half orphan forever.

"Found it!" Jay Jay holds up a white square of waxed cardboard.

I exhale as he puts it in my box. I don't want to look at him. If he's in my grade, we're going to be at school together in a couple of months. If he's one of the popular kids, this is going to be so bad.

Maybe by September he'll forget all about me.

Or maybe . . . "Do you live with your grandma?"

Maybe he's just visiting.

"Yeah," he says. "My mom and dad, they're kind of a mess. I haven't seen them in a long time."

I wince. I knew I shouldn't have asked. "I'm sorry."

"So I didn't even know your house was for sale," he says when the silence gets awkward.

I'm completely thrown off guard. "What?"

"You just moved in behind us? On the corner? I didn't know that family moved."

"Yeah," I say, finally looking up at him.

"I didn't even know that house was for sale."

"Oh. I don't think . . . I mean, my—Lila—grew up in it. I don't think it was for sale."

"You know Lila?"

"Yeah, she's my—" Nope. I still can't say it. "My dad married her."

"Your dad is married to Lila O'Neil?"

I don't even know my dad's wife's last name. I guess it's Hart now, but I don't know what it was before. "I think so."

"You *think* so?"

My face burns again. "It was pretty sudden. Do you know her?"

"Sure," he says. "I mean, if she's Lila O'Neil. Real pretty blond girl? Tall."

That's her. "Yeah."

"She's friends with my aunt Lucy," he says. "But she's only like twenty-two or something, right?"

"Twenty-three."

Jay Jay makes a little sound of understanding. "Well, tell her 'hey' for me."

"Yeah, sure." I can barely tell her "hey" for myself, but whatever. "I better go."

"You should come hang out with us tomorrow," Jay Jay says.

I look up at him, trying to decide if he's serious. "Why?"

He shrugs. "I figured you probably don't know anyone yet."

"But you think I'm a total freak now."

"I don't think that."

For some reason, I'm angry all over again. "Well, maybe you should. My dad and Lila do."

"Yeah?" He shrugs both shoulders and looks away from me, at the sand between his feet. "Well, I'm pretty sure that my mom only had me so she could make my grandma take care of a black kid."

Balance is restored so quickly that it makes my head spin. "What?"

He shrugs. It surprises me that he understands balance. He seems to know that the only way to make things okay is to say something that makes him as torn open as I feel right now. I have no idea how to respond to what he said about his mother and his grandmother, except to say, "You really think your mom did that?"

He shrugs again. "I don't know. Maybe not."

I stand up, holding tight to my box. "I really need to get home. My dad's going to lose it if he finds out I left."

"Oh." He seems disappointed. That makes me feel kind of good.

I left my only real friend a thousand miles away, and even though she didn't seem real upset about it, I miss her. And now that a maybe friend, a maybe-maybe one anyway, is standing right in front of me after dark, under the stairs on the beach, I'm afraid if I move, he might pop like a bubble.

"So. Want to hang out tomorrow then?" he asks, and everything slides back into the range of normal.

"Yeah." *Whatever, no big deal.* "Sure."

He looks around. "Want to meet me here?"

I have a maybe-maybe friend, and I'm meeting him tomorrow in a clubhouse. "Uh-huh."

"So, like nine or so?" he asks. "My grandma won't let me leave the house until after breakfast."

I start to walk around the stairs. Nine is early for summer, but I don't care. "That sounds okay."

He walks up to the bluff with me, and then across the street. He doesn't just go home. He waits at the corner while I walk toward Lila's house.

"Oh, hey!" he calls out. "Are you in Lila's old room?"

I turn back. "Yeah."

He points toward the back side of the Haunted Mansion. "See that window? The one on the tower thing?"

I look at it and nod.

"That's my aunt Lucy's bedroom." It's even more like

Rapunzel's tower than mine is. "She's in Oregon at school now, but they used to leave messages for each other in the windows. Maybe we can do that."

I nod again, because I'm not sure what to say.

"Okay," he says. "Night."

He stays there, though, and waits until I'm walking up the staircase back to the balcony outside Lila's old bedroom.

FIVE

After I sneak into the room that isn't really mine, I stop and listen. I don't hear anything from the bedroom below.

I'm not ready to think about what that means, so I decide that Dad and Lila are asleep or watching TV downstairs, even though I don't hear that either. I put on my pajamas and lie down. Since I know they're all there, I'm fine with putting my missing kids in order tomorrow.

I stay fine with that right up until I start to wonder about Lila. How long has my dad known her, anyway? I think about how he used to come home close to when I got out of school. Especially right after Mom died.

And then it was later, six before he got home.

Then seven. Then we were eating pizza for dinner at eight thirty.

Because he was with Lila.

After trying to sleep for an hour, I flip on the little lamp clamped to the edge of the changing table and sit up.

God, I'm homesick.

I miss Denver. I miss Megan and my soccer team. I miss

when everything in my life was normal. Not four days ago when we left Denver. Seven-hundred and fifty-eight days ago, before Mom got sick. I miss not feeling like anyone was just putting up with me. I miss not thinking about stupid milk cartons.

I reach for my soccer ball and lie back on the bed, throwing it up and catching it over and over while I get lost in a fantasy about running away.

Not *from* home. Running away *to* home.

Maybe Megan's parents would take me in. We're on the same soccer team. Or we used to be. And I pretty much spent as many nights at their house as I did at my own since kindergarten. At least until the whole milk-carton thing.

Maybe I can go back home and leave my milk-carton kids in Los Angeles. We'll be Meg and Tesseract again, instead of Megan and Half-Orphan Girl.

I get so caught up in my daydream that I miss the ball, and instead of landing in my hands, it bounces off my face and thuds to the hardwood floor.

I sit up and cover my mouth with my hand to keep from crying out. A little too late, though. A single squeal escapes me. It's not like I haven't taken a ball to the face before, but usually I'm at least somewhat prepared for it. And usually it isn't a direct hit to my nose.

I stay there for a few minutes, my nose throbbing. When I'm sure no one is going to come check on me, I reach for my milk-carton kids and the box of tissues that Lila left on the edge of the changing table.

I think about burying my shoebox in the sand at the beach.

Or pitching the cards, one at a time, into the surf. I imagine fish nibbling at the corners until the cardboard is gone. And then Lila buying the fish at the supermarket and making tacos out of them.

I take the stack of cards and place it on the bed. One card at a time, I pick them up and carefully brush them off. I say each name, repeat each statistic. Every ounce of information I can take from what the Center for Missing and Exploited Children has printed on the back of a milk carton.

I alphabetize the cards as I work. These kids are missing or exploited. Or both, I suppose. But in my shoebox, I put them where they belong.

Fat, quiet tears fall down my face, and my aching nose starts to run.

✳ ✳ ✳

When I wake up the next morning, my eyes are swollen. I can barely open them. And my nose feels weird and stiff from getting bopped by my soccer ball.

The little alarm clock on the desk in the closet says it's eight a.m.

"Perfect." I rub my hands gingerly over my eyes. Nothing like looking like a mess in front of people who already think you are one.

I sit on the floor and open my suitcase and try to decide what to put on. A sundress is too fancy. Jean shorts and a tank top is too *not* fancy. I finally decide on the shorts and a red-and-white-striped top Gran gave me for my birthday last year.

I don't have a mirror in my new bedroom, but I don't need one to know that I don't look like the girls on the cover of *Seventeen* magazine, like Lila does.

No one will ever describe me as tall and blond and pretty.

Dad says I look like Mom. That used to make me happy, even if I didn't really believe it. Mom wasn't mousy like me. She was beautiful.

I remember curling next to her in her hospital bed a few weeks before she died. She took my hand and ran her fingers along mine. She was so small. Like the Incredible Shrinking Woman. *See how our hands are the same, Tessa?*

They were. And my hair is the same color as hers, too. I have brown eyes like Dad, but they are round and wide set, like Mom's were.

* * *

Cold water from the bathroom sink doesn't do anything except feel nice. My eyelids are still red and puffy. I must have cried in my sleep half the night. At least my nose looks more normal than it feels. I get a washcloth wet and hold it against my eyes.

I finally accept that I'm not going to make myself look normal with cold water and a washcloth, so I pull my brush through my hair and wrestle it into a ponytail instead. I hesitate a minute, then pull the fistful of hair up higher and to the right, the way Lila wore hers the first time I met her.

"You are definitely not a model," I say to my reflection, but I pull an elastic band around the ponytail and keep it that way.

❋   ❋   ❋

"Morning," Lila says when I go into the kitchen. She's washing dishes. I feel even more tongue-tied around her than I did the day before. And, too late, I realize I don't want her to see that I've copied her hairstyle. I reach up for the elastic band, but she turns to see me before I can pull it out.

"Oh, cute!" She tilts her head. "I'll show you how to use my crimper, if you want."

"Oh. Uh . . . thanks." Apparently, my jaw is still rusty. I finally find the words to ask, "Where's my dad?"

"He's gone to meet with the principal at the high school."

"He's not here?" Dad left me with Lila and didn't even say anything? "When will he be back?"

"I'm not sure." Lila looks at my swollen eyes, then away from them. "Is there anything special you want to do today?"

Tears sting my burning eyes, and I hold the washcloth to them again, hiding behind the cool, wet terry cloth.

I'd planned on asking Dad if I can hang out with Jay Jay. I hate that I have to ask Lila instead. Not because I mind so much, but because I still haven't figured out *how* to talk to her.

"Tessa, what's wrong?"

Lila takes a step toward me, and I back up. "Can I go to the beach?"

Lila looks around the kitchen like maybe I'm asking someone else. She finally takes a breath and says, "I guess it's okay."

"Thanks." I head for the back door.

"Do you want me to go with you?"

My side ponytail thwaps my ear when I shake my head. I should tell her that I'm meeting Jay Jay, but instead I just say, "No."

"Hang on." She reaches into her pocket and brings out a five-dollar bill. "There's a little shop about two blocks up First Street that sells the best donuts I've ever had. I used to get one on my way to school every morning."

Right. Because she gets to live where she's always lived. Two blocks from her favorite donut shop.

I don't know what to do with her being nice to me. It makes me feel off-balance. I take the money and shove it into my back pocket, mumble something that kind of resembles *Thanks,* then turn and practically run out of the kitchen.

It's still almost an hour before I'm supposed to meet Jay Jay. I walk past his house, holding the wet cloth to my right eye and then my left.

I think about Jay Jay's green eye. Then his blue eye. Does he see the same through each of them? Do my brown eyes affect how I see the world? How would I even know?

Even in the daylight, his house looks haunted. It's huge. At least four times the size of Lila's house or any other house around it. Dark and creepy, covered with ivy and roses, and with a thousand windows and round turrets like a castle. It looks to me like it was here first, and then the other, newer, smaller houses snuck up on it and invaded its territory.

✳ ✳ ✳

I look at the window that Jay Jay said was his aunt Lucy's bedroom and wonder which one is his. I'm tempted to knock on the door and ask if he wants to come out early, but I don't have the nerve to risk looking so eager.

Instead, I walk across the street to the bluff. It was nearly deserted the night before, but this morning dozens of people walk or jog or roller-skate along the sidewalk. A lot of them have dogs on leashes. I head for the wooden staircase. I'll check out the clubhouse again before Jay Jay gets there.

Thinking about the clubhouse as I take the stairs down makes me think of the stairs leading down from the balcony outside my bedroom at Lila's house.

Maybe there's a way to soundproof the vent by my bed, so I won't have to hear them talking.

I stop about halfway down the stairs when I hear voices. There are people in the clubhouse. I rush the rest of the way down, heart pounding.

I have no idea what I'm going to do or say, but I'm ready for a fight. My hands are actually balled into fists.

Jay Jay looks up at me from one of the turned-over milk crates. There are three other boys with him. A chubby kid and a skinny one who both look our age, and a little boy who is a lot younger. Maybe a first or second grader. All four of them stare at me like I'm an alien from outer space or something.

They look perfectly comfortable. Like they belong here.

"This is *your* clubhouse?" I say to Jay Jay, surprised. I shouldn't have been. He was there last night. He *told* me it was a clubhouse. I don't know why I assumed that he'd just stumbled on it, like I did.

"It's *our* clubhouse," Skinny Kid answers. "Obviously."

Jay Jay stands up. "This is Tessa, guys."

He's already told them about me.

Chubby Kid stands up, and I think I'm definitely going to need names for them soon. He says, "And, for your information, you can't just come here whenever you want."

"Don't be a jerk, O." Jay Jay looks back at me and shakes his head. Calling the other boy a jerk was mean, but Jay Jay doesn't sound angry and the other kid doesn't seem upset. "Don't listen to Oscar."

Oscar wrinkles his nose, then sits again.

"I'm Petey," the skinny boy says. "This is my brother, Marvel."

"Your name is Marvel?" I look at the younger kid. He's got blond hair and freckles and looks more like a Mikey or a Tommy than a Marvel. I actually can't think of any kid outside a comic book who looks like a Marvel.

"Don't be rude," Oscar says.

I think about shooting that right back at him but change my mind. He's right, anyway; that was rude.

"Sorry."

"So, you escaped early this morning. Me too." Jay Jay tilts his head as he looks at me.

"Well." I don't want these kids to think I'm a prisoner in Lila's house or something. "My dad's at his new school, so I just—"

"My grandma's doing the windows today." Jay Jay looks at Oscar, then back at me. "Trust me, early is better on windows day."

Her house has more windows than I've seen on one house in

my whole life. I don't know how to respond, though, so it takes me a few seconds too long to say, "I bet."

Jay Jay leans forward, a little closer to me. "Are you okay?"

Oscar is watching me with black eyes that are impossible to read. Marvel is basically a tiny version of his older brother, and they're both staring at me, too.

I take a little step back. If I were home in Denver, I'd be so out of here. I'd have places to go. Home, for one thing. Or Megan's house. Or the park that's halfway to our school. Or the Pizza Plaza that's three streets away in the other direction. It has a Ms. Pac-Man machine that's actually a table and the best chicken wings on the planet.

But in California? There isn't anywhere for me to go except back to a house that isn't mine. My dad's not even there. I'd have to stay with Lila. I don't know anyone. I don't even know how to get to First Street where the stupid donut shop is.

Tears sting my eyes again and I hold the washcloth to them, wishing I could just disappear.

"What's wrong with her?" Oscar asks.

"Don't be a jerk, O," Jay Jay says again, and puts a hand on my shoulder. "Don't worry about him. He's not good with people. Seriously, we should keep him locked in a cage."

"Shut up," Oscar says. He still doesn't sound mad, though.

"Anyway. We're going to hit up the community center today." Jay Jay stands up. "You should come. They have foosball."

I feel a little knot release in the center of my chest. "You play foosball?"

The little clubhouse goes quiet, and a look passes between the four boys. Petey finally speaks up. "Yeah."

"Me too," I say. "I mean, I like to play. I used to a lot in Denver."

"Are you any good?" Jay Jay asks.

I'm better than Megan. Sometimes I could even beat Denny. But it feels like bragging to say so. I shrug. "I guess."

"The community center costs ten bucks for the summer," Oscar says, like he's hoping that I won't have ten dollars. And he's right. I don't. I reach into my pocket and pull out the five-dollar bill that Lila gave me.

Jay Jay asks again, "But you know how to play for real?"

"Yeah." I clear my throat and try again. "I mean. Yeah. I do. But I don't have enough money."

Jay Jay elbows Oscar, then pulls a red Velcro wallet out of his own back pocket and peels it open. The sound echoes in the little cave of a clubhouse. "I have two bucks."

When no one else says anything, he looks up and turns to Petey, who sighs and says, "I have a buck fifty, but it's supposed to be for . . ."

He looks at me and doesn't say what his money is for.

Jay Jay shoots Oscar another look.

"Oh my God. Fine." Oscar pulls a handful of change out of his left pocket and adds a pile of nickels and dimes and quarters to the pot. No one says anything, but I see Petey put his money back in his pocket.

Jay Jay and Oscar have given their snack money to me, and that makes me feel strange. I want to give the money back and say, *Never mind, I don't want to go to the community center with you*. But that would be a lie. Kind of. As much as I want to just walk away and get myself out of this awkward situation, I'm happy that Jay Jay wanted to keep me around today.

Plus, I really am good at foosball.

I want to show off. I want these boys to want me to be their friend. I wonder if they can feel how extremely desperate I am.

I am a sad, sad loser is what I am. That's the truth.

I take the money when Jay Jay offers it to me and stuff it in my pocket. I hear the ocean and a million people outside the clubhouse as we all stand under the stairs looking at each other.

"So, who has food?" Oscar finally asks.

Jay Jay, Petey, and Marvel all reach for backpacks I didn't notice before. Oscar has one, too. They rummage in their bags and a little pile of granola bars and fruit roll-ups builds on an upturned crate. Oscar adds a peanut butter sandwich wrapped in a plastic baggie.

The boys divvy the food up in some way that must make sense to them but doesn't really to me. Marvel gets both of the apples and the sandwich. Oscar gets the granola bars. Jay Jay and Petey split what's left evenly. Jay Jay looks at me, then grabs one of Oscar's granola bars and tosses it my way.

Oscar reaches to catch it in midair, but misses. "Hey!"

I'm about to offer the snack back, because this boy already hates me. Jay Jay stops me with a fruit roll-up and a little bag of pretzels from his own stash.

Oscar rolls his eyes and says, "Let's get our bikes."

"Do you have a bike?" Jay Jay asks.

I do. It's currently wedged against a wall of applesauce in

Lila's garage that looks more like a strange grocery store than a place to park a car.

I'll have to ask Lila to take off the padlock before I go in there. I wonder if I can find a way to just sneak my bike out without her knowing. Maybe the key is in a kitchen drawer or something.

It doesn't really matter, though. Even if I could get past the lock, my front tire is flat.

It surprises me that I really don't want these boys to see Lila's garage. Especially Oscar.

"You could get your cards, too," Marvel says. When Petey elbows him, he adds, "You know. If you wanted to."

Jay Jay told them.

Oscar's face lights up a little, and I wonder if showing him my collection will make him hate me less. It's doubtful that it will make him like me.

It's warm, but I wrap my arms around my waist, remembering the first time I stood in front of the milk case at school when I couldn't find a kid I didn't already have. The panic that built in me like Mount St. Helens and filled me up until I felt like I might erupt.

I pull the money back out of my pocket and reach it toward Jay Jay, including the five from Lila. "You guys go ahead. My dad wants me to unpack my bedroom anyway."

Jay Jay stares at my hand. He looks up at the others, and I feel sick to my stomach. I want to crawl under the sand, bury myself in it.

To my surprise, it's Oscar who talks. "This is so stupid. She can use Olivia's bike."

The other three boys stare at Oscar like he'd suggested I fly to the community center on my fairy wings. Jay Jay finally says, "Are you sure?"

"Who's Olivia?" I ask.

Oscar shoots me a look and leaves the clubhouse. Petey follows, with Marvel close behind him. Jay Jay waits, and I don't know what to do. I don't know what just happened.

"Olivia is Oscar's sister," Jay Jay says. "She died last year."

I push the money back into my pocket. "Really?"

"She had cancer. She was sick for a long time." Jay Jay follows the others. "It's a big deal that he's offered you her bike."

* * *

All of the boys have bikes at the Haunted Mansion. Jay Jay's grandmother sounds a little scary to me, but at least she lets Oscar and Petey and Marvel keep their rides in her massive garage.

"So how far away is your house?" I ask Oscar.

"About three miles."

Well, that's a long way to walk. I bite my bottom lip and look back toward Lila's house. Maybe I should just go get my own bike. I'm sure Lila would let me into the garage. Maybe Jay Jay has a pump.

But then I'd have to tell her where I was going and why and with who, and that's more words than I've ever said to her at once.

"Want to ride on my handlebars?" Jay Jay asks me.

"Um." I'm not real tall, but I'm also not small, like a lot of the girls at my school. I'm definitely not "ride on my handlebars" small. "I'm not sure."

Jay Jay shrugs one shoulder. "I have pegs. I won't let you fall."

I look down at his bike's front tire. Silver pegs jut out from either side—a place to put my feet and keep myself balanced on the handlebars. All of the boys are looking at me now. Oscar has this smirk, and I'm sure he thinks I'm going to chicken out.

The urge to keep him from seeing Lila's weird garage rears up again.

"Okay," I say. "I guess so."

Jay Jay straddles his bike and holds it steady while I stand with my back to him, the front tire between my legs. I put my left foot on a peg and the edge of my rear end against the handlebar. Before I do a little bunny hop and get myself up there, I wonder if my butt is going to look weird, squished against a metal bar.

"Come on," Jay Jay says. "I won't let you fall."

I put my weight on the left peg at the same time that I push off the ground with my right, and I'm up. I hold on to the handlebars tightly enough to hurt my fingers and lean back a little to keep my balance. Jay Jay leans forward, and I hear him laugh near my left shoulder before he kicks off and we're moving.

After a couple of awkward minutes, we're going fast enough for the ride to smooth out. Jay Jay and Oscar call back and forth behind me, but I'm too focused on the wind blowing my side ponytail and the hope that I don't fall over and kill myself to pay attention to what they're saying.

The farther we ride from the shore, the smaller and more closely packed the houses become. There are a lot of kids in Oscar's neighborhood, playing behind metal fences in front yards with swing sets and kiddie pools, or riding skateboards up and down the blacktop beside the sidewalk. A couple of them have set up a dangerous-looking homemade jump in front of a driveway.

Jay Jay veers toward the jump and says, "Want to try it?"

I shake my head, the end of my ponytail flapping against my face. "Oh my God, don't you dare!"

He laughs and rides past it.

Oscar's house is a neat little square, painted blue with white shutters, and a perfectly green, equally square front lawn. There are two wooden half-barrels full of geraniums, one on either side of the stairs leading up to the small front porch. It reminds me of a dollhouse.

Jay Jay slows, and I put my feet on the ground when he stops. He's breathing heavily behind me, and I want to apologize, but I can't get the words organized to come out.

The scale between us is unbalanced, and I hope that I'll have a chance to do something for him soon. For now, I just jump off the bike and say, "Thanks."

He lifts his chin like carrying me three miles on his handlebars was no big deal. Oscar sets his bike on its kickstand and goes to the top of his walkway. He looks at the front door for a moment, like he's trying to build up his nerve. He pulls a key from where it's hanging on a piece of string around his neck, under his T-shirt. Instead of taking the key off, he bends his knees and lowers himself so he can turn the lock and open the door.

Jay Jay, Petey, and Marvel all stand on the sidewalk, so I do, too. There's a quietness that surrounds Oscar's house, like a bubble. It blocks out the noise of the rest of the neighborhood. It muffles whatever sound the boys might have made. Or maybe it just seems that way, because the wind was blowing in my ears on the way here.

Marvel rocks back and forth, from heel to toe and back again. I think he's going to say something, complain about Oscar taking too long, but Petey puts a hand on his head and he stays quiet.

"Are Oscar's parents home?" I ask.

"It's just his mom. She's at my house." I look up at Jay Jay and he lifts his eyebrows. "She's my grandma's housekeeper. Don't you know? Only Mexicans know how to wash windows properly."

Jay Jay really doesn't seem to like his grandmother very much. I think she must not be anything at all like Gran. I don't even know how to respond to him, and luckily, I don't have to. The garage door finally opens, and I see Oscar standing at the back of the well-kept space. It's the exact opposite of Lila's garage.

He wheels out a bike. It's a yellow Beach Cruiser with fat tires and wide handlebars. A purple lock is wound around the frame. I take a step back.

What if I crash?

What if someone steals Olivia's bike while I'm borrowing it?

Jay Jay takes the bike, and Oscar goes back in before I can say anything. The garage door starts to slide shut. Jay Jay hands it over, and I take it to keep it from falling onto the sidewalk. "I don't think this is a good idea."

"It's okay," Marvel says. "Olivia would want you to ride it. She was really nice."

Jay Jay stands closer to me, watching me with his strange eyes. "Let Oscar do this. He usually won't even talk about her."

Maybe if I do this, it'll balance things again between us. When Oscar is back, the boys leave, and I get on his dead sister's bike and go with them.

The five-mile ride between Oscar's house and the community center is nice. It takes long enough for me to start to think about how strange it is that I've made some maybe-maybe friends already.

Probably because I don't have to choose a milk carton in front of these boys. If I go to school with them in the fall, I'm pretty sure they'll think I am a freak.

I mean, Jay Jay saw my cards and he told the others about them. They still wanted to hang out with me, but that's not the same as witnessing how I get them.

Jay Jay rides beside me but talks mostly to Oscar and Petey. Marvel rides behind us. His bike is smaller, and his legs are shorter, but when I look over my shoulder at him, he seems like he's holding his own.

The community center is a big, low building made of cinder block. It's surrounded by basketball and tennis courts and has a grassy playground. No one is playing tennis except for four women with white hair, but there's an intense game of basketball happening. High school boys play, half of them with their T-shirts in a pile on the ground. High school girls watch, sitting in bunches with their knees together, pretending like they're paying attention to anything but the boys.

I think they're totally paying attention to the boys.

Middle school kids probably never get to play basketball. Not that I care. I prefer soccer. But Jay Jay watches them as we ride by. We stop at a big metal rack and lock up our bikes in a row on one end.

"Do you ever play?" I ask him.

"Not this summer." He heads toward the building before I can ask any more questions.

There's a desk inside the front door, and a girl smiles at us as we walk in. She has a dark-brown ponytail and a green T-shirt with a rainbow iron-on decal and the words *It's a Sunny Day at the Greater Los Angeles Community Center* on the front. "Hey, guys."

"Hi, Jessica," Jay Jay says.

Jessica shifts her eyes to me, and her smile widens. She looks like it's her mission in life to make sure every kid feels welcome at the Greater Los Angeles Community Center. "New friend?"

"This is Tessa." Jay Jay pushes me forward a little, and I dig into my pocket for the wad of bills and handful of change. "She wants to sign up."

"What a pretty name." Jessica pulls a half sheet of pink paper from somewhere behind the desk. "Just need you to fill this out."

She plucks a pen with a huge yellow sunflower glued to the top from a red flowerpot on the counter and hands it to me. The paper just wants my name, my dad's name, and our address and phone number.

I print our names and the first two numbers of my address in Denver—and then my heart stutters and I pull the pen from the paper.

I don't look up, because I know they're all watching me. I don't want to admit that I don't know my address. It's not mine anyway. It's Lila's. It's Dad's and the new baby's. It's not mine.

I'm tempted to finish writing my old address in Denver, but some other kid lives in my old room now.

I scratch out the numbers and write *Second Street*, because I know that much. And as soon as those words are down, I remember seeing the big number 585 on the mailbox the night before and thinking that at least Lila's house had a satisfying number.

I hand the paper back without a phone number. No one's told me what it is in the new house.

Jessica doesn't seem to notice that I had a weird moment or that I left part of her form blank. She takes back her flowery pen and the pink paper and starts to count my money. She hands me back forty-five cents.

"All right, kiddo," she says. "You're set for a summer of fun."

"Great."

"Foosball awaits!" She waves us off, then goes back to a big book she has open in front of her. Some kind of school book, even though it's summer. She looks up again and says, "Snacks at ten thirty. We have chocolate chip cookies today, Marv."

Oscar, Petey, and Marvel have already started walking down a hallway. Marvel lets out a small whoop.

The idea of cookies catches me up.

Cookies mean milk.

Having friends was fun while it lasted.

* * *

If the basketball courts belong to the high schoolers, the game room is ruled by middle school kids. There are two foosball tables, a pool table, and a Ping-Pong table that some girls have covered with a sheet and are using as a fort. I see their feet and knees under the edges of the makeshift walls.

A guy about Denny's age, wearing the same T-shirt as Jessica, stands on one side of a foosball table with a short girl with a blond braid and an armful of plastic bracelets. He spins his players so hard, I'm half afraid they'll fly off their bar. The girl squeals, and the two boys on the other side of the table spin their own players and then throw their arms up and groan when the ball sinks.

Jay Jay shakes his head and says, "Spinning isn't allowed."

"But it's fun." The guy in the T-shirt spins his keeper again.

"We call next game!" Marvel slaps a hand on the edge of the table just as one of the younger boys slams his keeper against the table and misses a block.

"Game over!" The short girl dances a little. "We won!"

"You just walked in, Marv," another boy, leaning against the wall, says without moving. No one is playing on the other table, and I wonder why.

"So what? Did you call next game?" Marvel asks.

The boy hesitates, and Petey goes to the table. He waves Oscar over. "Come on, O."

Jay Jay looks at me and rolls his eyes. "Trust me, we need all the practice we can get."

"Go ahead," I say. "I'll watch."

"You sure you don't mind?" He's already at the table. Marvel bounces at his side, practically coming out of his skin.

I feel a little left out, but what exactly am I supposed to say? "It's fine."

"You can have next game," Jay Jay says. "Slap the table."

"What?"

He comes back to me, takes my hand, and slaps it down on the edge of the table. "Say 'next game.'"

"Next game."

"Good." He lets me go and takes his place next to Marvel. "Let's do this."

I stand for a few minutes and watch as Oscar drops the ball to start the game. They all go hyperfocused, bouncing on their toes and working their players. The ball shoots toward Marvel's defense, and he grunts and uses both of his palms to spin his players. I start to say something, but before I can, Jay Jay hip checks the younger boy and says, "You *know* spinning's illegal!"

Marvel's bottom lip pouts, but he stops spinning and the ball rolls to Jay Jay's offensive players. He shoots, hard, and scores.

Petey groans and says, "Get your head in the *game*, O!"

I wander away before Marvel drops the ball again. My head is still lost in Jessica's announcement of a snack that involves cookies and, probably, milk. If I can find the cafeteria, maybe I can see if Half-Orphan Girl's archnemesis lives there.

The milk cooler.

If there is one and I can find it, maybe I can look through it now, while the boys are occupied. I'll find a lost kid I don't already have and put that carton aside so I can pick it up and at least look like a normal person.

It's still weird, but it's secret weird. At least until I have to try to ride Oscar's sister's bike home with an old milk carton in my hand. I wish I'd thought to bring my backpack.

I leave the game room and head back to the hallway. I'll ask Jessica. Maybe make something up about an allergy or something. Need to inspect the cafeteria for rogue peanut butter.

Yeah, nothing weird there.

All I want in the world right now is to find out that the Greater Los Angeles Community Center only serves juice boxes.

There's a massive bulletin board lining one side of the hallway, covered in flyers advertising piano lessons and pooper scoopers and used cars for sale; business cards for local barbers and dentists and manicurists; pictures of kids at an aquarium, playing plastic recorders, running races.

There's a woman standing at the board. She's about my mom's age. In fact, she looks enough like my mom from the back to make me stop and stare. She's petite, with long, light-brown hair in a braid down her back, and she's dressed in nurse clothes— lavender scrubs and thick-soled white shoes.

She's looking at a flyer printed on lime-green paper with little strips cut at the bottom. Each strip has a telephone number written on it. She rubs her fingers together at her sides, like she's trying to stop herself from grabbing one of the strips.

As I pass, she turns and looks around. "Augie?"

I look around, too, and see a little boy, maybe four years old, come toward me from the front desk where I wrote the address that wasn't really my address on Jessica's pink page.

Jessica stops the nurse on the way out and says, "Don't worry, Mrs. Norton. I'm sure someone will call."

"Are you sure you can't help me out?" Mrs. Norton says. "I just need someone on Thursday afternoons."

"Oh, wow. I wish. I love Augie. But I've got work and summer school. I just can't."

Mrs. Norton picks up the little boy and walks out of the community center.

I look at the lime-green flyer she'd been staring at.

It reads: *Regular, responsible sitter needed for four-year-old boy every Thursday from 4:00 p.m. to 7:00 p.m.*

It's tacked next to a giant poster advertising the Third Annual Foosball-Palooza Tournament. Grand prize, in giant numbers, $1,000.

A thousand dollars for foosball?

There's a white sheet of paper at the bottom of the poster, with a pencil hanging by a string. A list of what looks to me like team names is listed on it, followed by the names of the kids on each team.

I run my finger down it until I get to an entry that says: *The Losers—Jay Jay Sampson, Oscar Montoya, Petey Lewis.* There's a name, *Aaron Casey*, that's scribbled out, and *Marvel Lewis* is written under it. My mouth tweaks into a half smile. For some reason, I love that they call themselves the Losers.

There's an envelope full of flyers with information about the tournament. I take one and fold it into quarters.

"Tessa?" I turn around. Jay Jay is standing in the doorway to the game room. "Want your turn?"

"What?"

"You slapped the table. You can take Marvel's place."

"You guys are doing this?" I lift the folded flyer.

Jay Jay's smile fades. "Yeah."

"The winner really gets a thousand bucks?"

"You know Andre Whittaker?"

My eyebrows lift. Andre Whittaker is only the most amazing soccer player. Ever. I saw him play once, when my dad took me to a game in Denver. "Sure."

"He's from around here. He sponsors the tournament. It's huge."

I shove the flyer into my back pocket. "Cool."

"So, ready?"

"Yeah."

"Hey, Tessa." I turn and see Marvel standing in the doorway to the game room. "I'll take your place if you want."

"I'm coming."

"The Losers are going to win this thing," Petey is saying as I follow Marvel and Jay Jay back into the game room. He's strutting like a crow. "We're going to kick *butt*."

"Not if we play like we just did," Oscar says.

"Don't be such a loser." Jay Jay pushes Oscar's shoulder with one hand.

"We *are* Losers, nutjob."

Jay Jay takes Marvel's place at the Foosball table and waves me over to the offensive spot. He doesn't look at me, though. He keeps talking to Oscar. "Don't be the wrong kind of loser, O. We *are* going to kick butt."

I wonder if he thinks he's doing me a favor, taking over the goal. Or if he just thinks a girl can't play defense. I wait until he looks at me, then ask, "Can I take the keeper?"

For a second, I can tell he's going to say no. I'm still not totally sure why. Offense is his position, after all. Or at least it was when he was playing with Marvel. But then he shrugs and moves down the table.

I open and close my hands, trying to relax them. "You guys call yourselves the Losers?"

"Why not?" Petey spins his players, even though there's no ball on the table. "Everyone else does."

I bounce on the balls of my feet and say, "Okay, let's go."

Marvel stands on his toes and leans over to drop the ball in the center of the table. I roll the bar, controlling my defenders, swinging their feet forward and back, as Oscar whacks it toward my goalkeeper. I connect and send the ball careening up to Jay Jay's offense.

"Holy crap," Jay Jay says under his breath. Petey frantically works his keeper, but Jay Jay is faster and sends the ball into the goal.

Marvel drops the ball again, and Oscar gets control of it. I move my hands to my keeper's bar and block his attempt at a goal. I knock it to my defense, then up to Jay Jay, who is almost too busy staring at me to react fast enough. He recovers, though, and sinks a second goal.

Marvel retrieves the ball, but Oscar puts a hand on his arm to stop him. "What is this?"

"What?" I ask, suddenly embarrassed.

"Are you some kind of prodigy or something?"

Heat rushes up from my chest, over my face. "Do they have foosball prodigies?"

Maybe I should have pretended that I hadn't spent hours playing foosball with Megan and Denny in their basement. If we had a team in the tournament, I think, we would have called ourselves the Wrinkles in Time. And we would have won.

"You are so on our team," Jay Jay says. "Holy crap, you're our secret weapon!"

"I am?"

"Hell yes, you are!" Oscar says. "Sorry, Marv. You're out."

Marvel's face screws up, his pale eyebrows burrowing down, his mouth scrunching. "Not fair."

"Don't worry," Petey says, wrapping an arm around his little brother and scrubbing his knuckles into the boy's crew cut. "You'll be our water boy."

"Our mascot!" Jay Jay says. He looks back at me and shakes his head. "Oh man. They'll never see a girl coming."

Story of my life. "Are we going to five?"

"Five?"

"Goals? How long does our game last?"

"Right. To five."

Marvel looks so sad, but he lifts his chin and reaches for the ball again. The exhilaration of the first part of our game evaporates as fast as it came. I'm left with a headache that I rub with my fingertips. "Okay."

Jay Jay puts a hand out to stop Marvel from dropping the ball. "What's wrong?"

I look around. All of the Losers are watching me. Another group of boys stands nearby, waiting for their turn and getting antsy because we're not playing. I have no idea why they don't play on the other table. Maybe it's broken. "I feel bad, taking Marvel's spot."

"It's okay," Marvel says. "Really. We need you on the team."

Jay Jay's face turns serious again, and he says, "Drop the ball, Marv."

SIX

Good thing: Once I am deep into foosball, I forget all about snack time.

Bad thing: Just as Jay Jay sinks the fifth goal in our fourth game, the guy in the *Greater Los Angeles Community Center* T-shirt—the one who reminds me of Denny—stands in the game room doorway and says, "Okay, snack time," and reminds me again.

My stomach curdles, like it's full of sour milk.

I could just sit it out. Go hide in the girls' bathroom.

For a few seconds I think, *Yeah, that could work.*

But not forever.

If I couldn't sit it out in Denver, I sure can't here. If there are milk cartons, I need to see if there's a kid that I don't have in my collection.

It doesn't matter that I don't want to.

* * *

I follow the boys as they start out of the game room, and I'm about to veer off toward the girls' bathroom anyway, because I might at least be able to be last in line, but Jay Jay grabs my arm before I can and says, "I think we might actually be able to win this thing."

"There are only two foosball tables," I say. "How big of a tournament could it be?"

"Oh no," Oscar says, behind me. "It's a huge thing. They set up a dozen tables in the basketball gym down at the Boys and Girls Club. There's TV cameras and everything."

"TV?"

"Sure. And Andre Whittaker is there. Every community center in the city has teams. Us. The Boys and Girls Club. The Y. And that's just this area."

"It's only local news," Jay Jay says. "But Andre Whittaker really will be there. He shakes every player's hand. Want to eat outside?"

Marvel reacts like someone just suggested math homework or a root canal. He says, "But we might get first turn at foosball."

Jay Jay looks at me again, then back at Marvel, who has lost interest because Jessica is handing him a little blue bag full of tiny chocolate chip cookies.

Beyond Marvel I see the one thing I hoped wouldn't be there. A big silver cooler full of pint-size milk cartons.

"Why couldn't it have been juice boxes?"

"What?" Jay Jay looks where I'm looking.

Maybe there are entirely different lost kids on West Coast milk cartons, and the first one I pick up will have a picture I've never seen before.

I'm not super hopeful of that, though. The whole point is

to spread the kids' faces all over the country so someone, some-where, might see them. I have kids in my box from every part of America.

I take the bag of cookies when Jessica hands it to me.

Unfortunately, all of the milk cartons have been arranged so the cow faces forward and the kids face backward. Oscar picks up a carton without even turning it over, and I feel almost sick with a mix of jealousy, that he can do that, and anxiety, over whether or not he has a kid I don't have.

Jay Jay picks one next. He palms the carton and looks back at me, then slowly turns it over, and I see a face I instantly rec-ognize.

I reach for a carton, turn it, and put it back. Again. Again. Raheem. Jocelyn. Sharona. I know those kids. I have them in my shoebox in the cubby over the bed that isn't really mine, in the room that isn't really mine, in the house that's not really mine *or* my dad's.

An older kid reaches over me and picks up Jocelyn. "They're all the same. Just take one."

They aren't. They aren't remotely all the same. I pick up another carton, hoping it's a kid I've never seen before.

I glance up at Jessica, who is definitely watching me now.

Please, don't make me stand here with my new friends staring at me and kids I don't know getting frustrated behind me and Jessica starting to notice how weird I am.

Please.

The milk carton has Elizabeth Dixon's five-year-old face on it.

Jay Jay asks, "Are you okay?"

I tighten my fingers around the carton in my hand, and I'm stuck. I want to just take it and go outside with Jay Jay and the others. But there might be a kid in the milk case that I don't have yet.

I put it back and start turning cartons again. Fast. I've done this before. Lots of times. Everyone will know, now, that I'm a total freak.

Before Jessica can step in, though, I finally find a boy I don't have. He's older, fifteen, with a mop of dark hair and brown eyes. His name is Seth.

Jay Jay doesn't seem to notice my panic. He says, "Ready?"

Oscar, Petey, and Marvel stand by the door that leads outside. They aren't paying attention to me at all. When I look back, Jessica has returned to handing out her little blue bags. The line is moving again, and I think, *Maybe I won't lose these maybe-maybe friends quite yet.*

✳ ✳ ✳

Marvel runs ahead and slaps his hand down on the top of a wooden picnic table that's attached to a tree with a big chain. Apparently, hand slapping is the dibs tool of choice in Los Angeles. He tears open his cookies while the rest of us catch up.

"Do I get a costume?" he asks.

Petey sits beside him. "Costume?"

"If I'm mascot. Duh."

"Sure," Jay Jay says. "We'll find you something awesome."

"So, why exactly are we giving first ups on the foosball table to the enemy?" Oscar looks at me like he's sure it's my fault.

"Don't be a jerk, O," Jay Jay and Petey say at the same time.

"Don't you think we need to evaluate our game plan?" Jay Jay asks.

"All right." Oscar pops a cookie and chews carefully. "So she's good. I'll give her that."

"She's not good," Petey says. "She's great!"

He says it like Tony the Tiger on the Frosted Flakes commercials, lifting one pointer finger toward the sky, and a burning blush raises over my face.

"Fine. But what was that thing at the milk case?" Oscar asks me.

I thought I was clear for today, except for the whole trying to ride a bike all the way home with a milk carton in one hand thing, so I am caught off guard. I swallow wrong and cookie crumbs lodge in my throat, making me hack up a lung.

Petey thumps me on the back while I cough until my face is as hot as a sunburn and my still-aching eyes stream tears down my cheeks.

"Jeez," Petey says. He hands me his milk carton, still half full, so I can take a drink.

Even after all that, I might have been okay if the cow side was facing me. But instead, I see a little girl with blond braids and a name I don't recognize.

Please, no. This is not going to happen.

You are not going to try to take home everyone's milk cartons, Tessa Hart. You are not.

In Denver, it was bad enough that I couldn't get rid of my own carton. At least I never tried to hoard anyone else's. But no one had ever handed me one with a kid on it that I didn't have already. And after a while it was hard enough to find one kid I didn't have, much less happening to see another one on someone else's carton.

I'd thought about searching tables and trash cans if I couldn't find one—but this was different. I close my eyes and tighten my fingers around Petey's carton.

"Are you okay?" Marvel asks. "You don't look so good."

"I'm fine."

"So are you going to tell us or what?" Oscar sits across from me at the picnic table and leans forward on his elbows.

I expect Jay Jay to tell his friend to stop being a jerk again, but he doesn't. Instead, he stands behind Oscar and looks at me like he's expecting an explanation, too.

"It's not a big deal," I say.

Oscar reaches for Petey's milk carton, and I pull it out of reach. "Right. Until we let you on our crew and Marvel stops practicing—and you go all guano crazy on us."

"Guano?"

"Bat poop," all four boys say.

"Sorry, Tessa." Jay Jay sits beside Oscar. "We do need to know what's going on."

"I told you it's nothing."

Oscar pulls his own milk carton in front of him and turns it around, so the kid faces me. I moan softly. I had to turn over twenty milk cartons to get one that was new to me—but both Petey and Oscar managed to find kids I didn't already have without even trying.

Life is colossally unfair.

Oscar sees it in my face, and he tilts his head. "So, if it's no big deal, you won't mind if I just . . ."

He takes his carton in both hands and slowly starts to squish its sides.

I last until the little boy's face starts to collapse and then I lean forward and grab the carton out of his hand.

What if I never find this kid again?

It isn't rational to believe that if I memorize the boy's stats, whisper his name every night before I go to bed, look at his picture until I know it like I know the faces in my sixth-grade yearbook—if I do all that, he'll be safe.

He'll be found and returned to his family that must be frantic with fear and worry for him. It's happened before.

"They found one of these kids," I say. "In Colorado, a few months ago. It was on the news."

"That's great. I mean, good for him, and all," Jay Jay says. "But what does that have to do with anything?"

"Not him. Her." Amanda Lansing was the first kid I collected. I saw her on my milk carton at lunch on a random Tuesday, and I don't know why, but I couldn't throw her away. I just couldn't. The idea of dumping her into the huge black trash bin near the door to the school's courtyard made me feel sick.

So I kept the carton. I took it into the bathroom by the gym, and I opened the top and used powdered hand soap to clean it out.

Hillary MacLean walked in and said, *Hey, Cinderella, you don't actually have to* wash *the trash before you take it out.*

I felt sick to my stomach that day. But I still carried that milk carton home and used Mom's dish soap and her little bird scissors to wash and trim it.

And I looked at Amanda Lansing for three days.

Then I went to Gran's for dinner on Saturday. She eats early and watches the news at six every night of her life.

We have breaking news at this hour. Amanda Lansing, missing since November, was found in Boulder last night after police followed a tip from a resident who saw the eleven-year-old girl at a local grocery store. The sighting was reported on Friday afternoon, and police located the girl in a hotel room with her abductor.

"I didn't throw away her milk carton, and they found her."

Oscar leans back away from me.

"But come on," Petey says. "They didn't find her because you had her milk-carton picture. I mean, unless you're the one who saw her and called the cops."

"I know that." And I do. I know it. But it doesn't matter. I still can't throw those kids away. And now I have no idea how I'm going to ride a bike with three milk cartons.

"So what?" Jay Jay asks. "You really believe that if you collect those kids, they'll be found?"

Even Megan never asked me that. I told her about Amanda Lansing, and she never asked me about the milk cartons. I'm so off balance that it actually feels like the world is tilting. "I know it's stupid."

Jay Jay lifts his eyebrows and gives Petey a look I don't understand. "I've heard of stupider stuff."

Petey leans over the table and shoves Jay Jay's shoulder. "It's not stupid."

They're not talking about my milk cartons anymore. "What?"

"Nothing," Oscar says. "It's just . . . nothing."

He nearly crushes his milk carton for real, but Marvel stops him. The little boy snatches it out of his hand and gives it to me.

"Thanks," I say.

"I'll carry them in my backpack if you want."

Everyone is staring at me. I'm grateful to Marvel, but the unbalance is almost unbearable. I say *Thanks* under my breath.

"Marv—" Petey starts to say something.

"It could happen," Marvel says. "Maybe it really could."

He takes all three cartons and goes back into the building. My heart lurches a little, but I'm able to let him go.

"We have to win the tournament," Oscar finally says. "We truly do."

I sense the opportunity to restore balance and can't help myself. "Why?"

"There's a thousand-dollar prize," he says.

I take the flyer out of my back pocket and spread it open on the table. "So how does it work?"

"We play on Friday," Jay Jay says. "The top-ten teams play elimination rounds in the finals the next Friday. If we win one in the finals, we move on to the next until there are just two teams left. And then just one winner."

"Wait. You mean *this* Friday?"

"Yep," Jay Jay says. "Starts at ten a.m. at the Boys and Girls Club."

The tournament starts two days after tomorrow, and I wonder how we could possibly practice enough to even make it to the second day of competition. Maybe we could do well next year, but this weekend? "How far did you get last year?"

"We didn't play last year."

Jay Jay looks at me, and I find my eyes shifting from his blue eye to his green one. I don't even know what to say. "Okay."

"Anyway," Petey interrupts before I can ask anything else. "That's two-fifty each. Who wouldn't want to win that?"

Oscar lifts his shoulders. "It's a frickin' fortune."

But he gives the other boys a look. There's more to the story, and even if they aren't going to tell me now, it restores some balance just knowing that it's there.

"Awww . . ." The voice comes from behind me, and I look over my shoulder at a boy with hair the color of carrots. "It's the Losers table."

Jay Jay rolls his different-colored eyes.

Oscar says, "That's right. So go away, Ricky."

"Go away, Ricky," the boy mimics.

Petey stands up. "Marv already slapped the table. Let's do this."

Ricky reaches over me and snaps up the flyer. "I don't know why you losers are bothering to even try. We're going to win this. Everyone knows we're going to win this. You won't make it to the finals."

Another boy, this one taller and heavier, shoves Ricky's shoulder and sends him crashing into me. "Take a chill pill, Rick."

The only way for Ricky to right himself is to put his hand on my arm and push himself up. He starts to, but the new kid grabs him by his striped T-shirt and hauls him away from me before he can.

"Sorry," Ricky says to me.

"This is Aaron." Jay Jay lifts his chin toward the other kid. "Ex-Loser."

Aaron puts a hand over his heart, like it's been wounded. He has dishwater-blond hair and green eyes that are magnified behind a pair of thick glasses. "Marvel's holding the table for you. Move it or lose it, current Losers."

"Cute," Jay Jay says under his breath. He starts toward the building, and Oscar and Petey follow. So do I.

"What's an ex-Loser?" I ask Petey.

"He used to be part of our crew," he answers without looking at me. "He's not anymore."

"Why not?"

"God, you ask a lot of questions," Oscar says. Then he raises his voice, just as he starts into the building. "Because he's greedy and selfish, that's why!"

I look over my shoulder. Ricky is cracking up, laughing so hard he has to lean against the table to stay on his feet. Aaron watches us without even a smile.

* * *

A group of girls is playing on the one foosball table everyone plays at. Marvel bounces on his toes nearby, waiting for one side or the other to get to five.

"You guys are too slow," he whines. "We lost our turn. But I slapped it again."

I go to the other table and give one of the bars a spin. The little men rotate, just like they're supposed to. I reach my fingers into the pocket, but there's no ball.

"We never use this table," Jay Jay says, standing on the opposite side, his fingers gripping two of the bars.

"Why not?"

He looks surprised for a second. "Just no one ever does."

"Used to be for the staff," a kid who's maybe a year or two older than us says. "Remember? Stupid Ellis never let us play on it."

There's some murmuring of memory.

I'm not sure where it comes from, but I feel a burst of bravery. "So is there a ball?"

Jay Jay feels in the pocket on his side, then shakes his head. "Jessica probably has one."

"I'll go ask!" Marvel darts out of the room before anyone can stop him.

"Truly, no one plays on this table," Oscar says.

"So . . ." I tilt my head, looking at him. "It's the Losers table, then?"

He dips his chin and raises his eyebrows at my bad joke. "Even the Losers don't use it."

I toy with the keeper on my side. "Seems like a waste."

Oscar looks at Jay Jay, who raises both shoulders. "Would it be cheating?"

Marvel comes barreling back in, holding a small white ball up in one fist. "Got it!"

Petey and Oscar look at each other for a second, but then they take their spots and Jay Jay comes around next to me. The other kids in the room are watching now. The girls have even stopped playing.

The surge of nerve I felt earlier leaves when I hear Ricky say, "Now what are you losers doing?"

"They're playing on the other table," one of the girls says.

Aaron comes from behind him and walks up to the good table. He slaps his hand down on it and says, "Next game."

"Go ahead," Marvel says. "We don't need that table anymore anyway."

I expect someone to slap the Losers' table, to take the game after ours, but no one does.

Jay Jay says, "Drop the ball, Marv."

✳ ✳ ✳

The Losers have a rival crew: Ricky and Aaron, and two others— identical twin brothers with dark hair and eyes. While they wait for the girls at the good table to finish their game, one of them snorts and says, "They replaced the baby with a *girl*. Losers."

Marvel slaps our table with the palm of his hand and says, "You know what? *I* get next game."

I'm about to say that I'll be the mascot for the next round, but Petey puts his hand on his brother's shoulder and bends to whisper something in the little boy's ear.

Marvel's small face darkens.

"If Marvel wants his spot back, it's okay with me," I say. "Really. Or we could share it."

Marvel's blue eyes narrow when he looks at me. "No, it's fine."

"Are you sure?"

"Let's play," Oscar says.

There's no time to argue. Jay Jay passes the ball up to my defense, and I shoot it, hard, down the line to the other goal.

I have to admit, we play like a well-oiled machine. Petey and Oscar win this time, but it's close. Even the boys waiting their turn stop heckling and watch.

"If we're playing against other teams in the tournament," I ask, "don't we only need two players?"

"We take turns. There are six rounds on Friday. Three for O and Petey. Three for me and you," Jay Jay answers. "Everyone gets six games, even if they lose."

"We won't lose." Petey looks at Ricky and Aaron still leaning against the wall. "We can't."

SEVEN

On the ride home, I try to pay attention so I can remember the route. It's hopeless, though. I'll never make it back to the community center without the boys. Not after just one trip there and back.

When we finally get to our neighborhood, the boys all stop on the sidewalk between Jay Jay's house and mine.

"Why don't you guys come to my house?" Jay Jay says to Petey. "You can stay over. My grandma won't care."

"We gotta get home." Petey doesn't sound happy about that.

Marvel has deflated completely. He looks half the size he's been all day. "Are you sure?"

Petey puts a hand on his brother's shoulder. "Mom said we have to."

Marvel shrugs his brother's hand off.

"Wait." Everyone looks at me, like I popped out of the sewer drain or something.

"What?" Oscar says.

I rub my hand on my shorts, trying to dry my palm. "Sorry. Marvel has my . . ."

My voice trails off, but Marvel swings his backpack off his shoulders and unzips it. He pulls out one of the cartons and hands it to me, then another, and another.

"Thanks," I say.

Marvel nods and looks at his brother. The two of them ride off.

I still need to get Oscar's sister's bike to his house, but I'll climb up the stairs and leave the cartons on the balcony, I think. I'm definitely bringing my backpack tomorrow, if they want me to go with them again.

"Hang on," Oscar says just as I'm about to say that I'll be right back. "Just wait here."

He parks his bike on Jay Jay's driveway and walks in the front door like he owns the place. I've got my fingers in the drinking spouts of the milk cartons and that Neo-Maxi-Zoom-Dweebie feeling is back. Huge.

Jay Jay stands on the sidewalk with me and looks out toward the beach across the street. "You killed it today, by the way."

I shrug one shoulder. "I had fun."

"Are you going to come with us again tomorrow?"

I feel something let go in the center of my chest that I didn't realize was tight. "Yeah. I mean, if you want me to."

"We have to win that tournament," he says.

"Foosball?" As soon as the word is out of my mouth, I feel like an idiot. What other tournament? "Oh, right."

"It's a thousand bucks," Jay Jay says.

"Yeah. I know." I still have the flyer in my pocket, and we had a whole discussion about it at snack time and another during the lunch break.

He finally turns to me, and he looks fierce. Like a warrior. I take a half step back. "We *have* to win it."

"But why is it so important?"

Before he can answer, Oscar comes back out with a woman who, I think, must be his mother. She's very small, with black hair pulled back into a twist behind her head. She wears a light-blue dress and white sneakers. Oscar says something to her, then comes to us.

"Mom says we can leave Olivia's bike here, so you can use it again." He gives me a look that lets me know that he expects me to arrange my own ride. Soon. "If you have to."

"So, tomorrow?" Jay Jay asks me.

Both boys look at me and I say, "Yeah. Tomorrow."

※ ※ ※

The streetlights pop on practically the second I step foot on the front stoop of Lila's house. The timing is super satisfying and I smile. Before I can make a decision between knocking and just walking inside, the door opens.

"Oh God, Tessa." Lila takes a step back and covers her mouth with her hand.

She's been crying. Like, really crying, the way I had been in my sleep the night before. For a split second, I think *Dad's dead*. He's been in an accident or something. It's like the oxygen has been sucked from the universe and I can't draw a breath.

But then, her face melts in relief. She grabs me by my shoulders and shakes me once, hard enough to make my head snap back and the cartons on my fingertips rattle together. "Where have you been? Where were you?"

"I—" I yank away from her. "You said I could go out."

"That was *ten* hours ago!"

I step back from her. "I got home before the streetlights came on."

"Streetlights?" She looks at me like I've lost my mind.

Be home before the streetlights come on has been my rule since the third grade. It literally did not occur to me until that moment, with Lila standing in front of me trying to pull herself together, that it wasn't my rule in Los Angeles.

No. No, it *is* my rule in Los Angeles. I'm sure of it. She just doesn't know the rules. "Where's Dad?"

She wraps her arms around her huge, pregnant belly. "He went to orientation at the high school. For his new job."

"He got the job?" She nods. It bothers me to get that news from her. "When is he coming home?"

"Soon," she says, but she's still looking at me like I've kidnapped her puppy or something. "Why are you doing this to me?"

Doing this to *her*? I push past her and stomp toward the stairs. The words come tumbling out of me, though. "It's not my fault you don't know the rules. My mom would have known that I wasn't late until the streetlights came on."

She looks younger when she feels sorry for me—this little half orphan she's somehow gotten herself put in charge of. Like she wishes, maybe, that her own mom was there to help her deal with me. "I'm doing the best I can."

101

Meanness brews in me, like the coffee that bubbles in the top of Dad's coffee maker every morning. I don't want it to, but it comes spilling out of me. "You are not doing the best you can! You could have stayed away from my dad. You could have left us alone. We were happy in Denver."

"Tessa." We both turn to the front door. Dad is standing there holding a folder full of papers. I actually take a step forward before he closes the gap between himself and Lila and folds her up against him. "What's going on?"

Before Lila can answer, I run up the stairs and close myself in the bedroom that isn't even mine.

I have time to pace the length of the room twice before I hear footsteps and there's a knock on the door. I go to it, expecting to see Dad there. I expect him to hug me and tell me that we'll figure things out. Everything will be okay. Just give Lila some time.

And I'll tell him to forget it. I hate her. I don't *want* to give her some time. I want to go *home*. Right now.

I'm so sure I know what's going to happen, that when I open the door and it's Lila standing there, the breath goes out of me.

God. She's even pretty when her face is all red and puffy.

"Can I come in?" Lila asks, even though she's already standing in the doorway. And it's really her room, anyway.

"It's your house."

She runs her hand through her hair. It falls like strands of gold silk, and I have a momentary fantasy about cutting it off while she sleeps, the way that Cathy Dollanganger's grandmother makes her brother cut hers off in *Flowers in the Attic*.

"I was really worried," Lila says. "You can't just take off all day and not tell me where you are. You didn't call or check in or anything."

"Yeah. Well, I don't know the number." I walk around her, toward the door. "Where's Dad?"

"He went to pick up pizza."

I blink up at her, as stunned as if she'd slapped me. "He left?"

"Tessa."

I take a breath. "Do you have a bike pump?"

"What?"

"Is there a bike pump I can borrow? My tire's flat, and I need my bike tomorrow."

She looks back over her shoulder, like she's wishing as hard as I am that Dad was there. "Yeah, sure. I mean. I have one. You can use it."

"Thanks."

"Look, Tessa." She's not giving up. "I'm sorry I yelled at you, but you scared me half to death."

I do not want to comfort Lila. Ever since I learned that she even existed, I've tried to pretend that she wasn't real. Now I can't have that fantasy anymore.

I want my dad.

I want my *mom*. Every time I look at Lila, I want my mom so bad it hurts.

I wonder if the kids whose pictures are in my box feel the same way, wherever they are.

* * *

Dad comes home with a plain cheese pizza and makes us all sit around the kitchen table, like a normal family eating dinner. He won't let me take my paper plate upstairs or get away with saying I'm not hungry.

"Where's the pepperoni?" I ask.

"Lila doesn't like it."

"I like it just fine." Lila puts a slice on her plate. "It doesn't like me. Gives me heartburn."

Gross. "Fine. But, Dad, can you please tell Lila that I'm allowed to stay out until the streetlights come on?"

Dad takes a bite of his pizza. "That's the rule. But this is a new city. And it's a much bigger city than Denver."

"Denver's big."

Dad's eyebrows shoot up. "Lila would like you to let her know where you're going to be. And for you to check in. I think that's reasonable, don't you?"

I sit back in my chair and cross my arms over my chest. Lila sits beside my dad, too close.

"Fine," I finally say. "I'll call from the community center tomorrow."

"I'm not sure you should go anywhere tomorrow," he says.

It's been so long since he's tried to give me any rules that it takes me a minute to realize that he's talking about grounding me. "What?"

And then Lila and I both say at the same time, "No!"

We look at each other.

Lila clears her throat and asks, "Is that where you were today?"

"Yes."

"It's at least five miles away. How did you get there?"

"I met the boy who lives behind you."

Dad and Lila both give me blank looks, and I roll my eyes.

"Jay Jay?" Lila asks.

I'm not sure what to make of the fact that she knows him. Somehow, I thought he was just mine, even though he knew who she was, too. And his aunt is her friend. "Yes. His friend Oscar lent me a bike."

"Well," Dad says, "that was nice of him. But you should have told Lila where you were going, and I still think—"

"Jay Jay and Oscar are nice kids," Lila says quickly. "I just need to know where you are, is all. If your dad isn't here."

I take a bite of my pizza. "You're not my—"

"Stop." Dad takes my plate from me, leaving me holding my slice. He gives me a look that makes me shrink back into my seat.

"You can go tomorrow," Lila says quietly, overriding my dad, which gives me a lot to think about.

"And you'll check in," Dad prompts.

"Fine."

Negotiations over, Dad gives me back my plate.

✳   ✳   ✳

After dinner, I stand up and start to clear my place. Dad catches my arm, though, as I pass by him and says, "Let's go check out your bike, Cookie."

For a second, it's like old times. Like when Dad and I used to do things together while Mom was working a night shift at the VA hospital.

Lila smiles like she's part of it, and I steel myself for hearing Dad include her, but he just takes my plate and hands it to her, then steers me toward the front door.

Good. For a little while, anyway, I have my dad back, and I don't want her to take that from me. I don't want to share.

✳ ✳ ✳

The garage is packed to the ceiling with *stuff*. I stare down an aisle of gray metal shelves that are lined with boxes of cereal, cornbread mix, shampoo, laundry detergent. I spot at least a dozen bottles of that orange dish soap.

"What—" I don't even know what to say.

"Lila likes to be prepared," Dad says. "She cuts out coupons."

"Coupons?"

He shakes his head, standing next to me and taking in the stockpiles, too. "Stay here."

He heads into the controlled chaos and comes back rolling my bike. He's got a tire pump stuck under his arm and his small red toolbox balanced on the seat.

I feel like my whole world has contracted in on itself. Like a big fist has crushed the sides of it, the way Oscar crushed his milk carton earlier.

Dad doesn't notice. He pops the kickstand on the bike and says, "I want to check the brakes and chain for you, too."

I stand and watch him tune up the bike, adjusting things here and there. He's still dialed into the Afterschool Special where Tessa and her daddy have a very special bonding moment.

"So what are you doing at the rec center?" he asks. "Shooting some hoops?"

"Foosball," I say. "We're playing foosball."

"Oh yeah? You play a lot with Megan, right?" *Well, I* used *to.* I think about telling him about the tournament, but before I can, he keeps talking. "Or was that pinball?"

"No," I say. "It was foosball."

He finishes patching my front tire, puts air into it, then closes the toolbox and stands up. He looks at me and takes a breath.

Whatever anger I have melts when he pulls me into him for a hug. I wrap my arms around him, and I'm on the verge of telling him everything about my milk-carton kids and my new maybe-maybe friends and the tournament.

I can actually *feel* the relief before it even comes. It will be like popping a balloon that has inflated inside me.

But before I can say anything, Dad kisses the side of my head and says, "I need you to cut Lila a break, okay?"

I pull back and look up at him.

I can't get any words out, and Dad must take that as a good sign, because he gives me a smile like we're in on something together, although it doesn't quite reach his eyes.

He ruffles my hair. "It won't hurt to check in with her during the day, will it? I'll be getting set up at the high school for the next couple of weeks. There's a conference the principal wants me to go to next weekend. But I promise, things will be better after the baby is here."

What planet does he live on, anyway?

As he's lowering the door he says, "You're all set for tomorrow."

He leaves me staring after him.

✳ ✳ ✳

We spend an awkward evening watching *E.T.* on Lila's VCR.

"I bought it with money I got from sending in box tops," she says, patting the machine after pushing play. "Can you believe it?"

I can. She must have roughly a million of them. I had no idea that box tops were worth money. And I don't care. I'm still stuck on the revelation that we both have a thing about saving garbage.

How is it weird that I have a box of milk-carton kids, but not weird that she sends trash in the mail and gets money back?

Dad won't let me go to bed. He makes microwave popcorn and sits beside Lila on the sofa. She balances the bowl on her huge belly.

I want to puke.

At least I love *E.T.* It's my favorite movie, which is probably why we're watching it. Dad is quietly bribing me to be nice to Lila.

The movie hits me harder than usual. I feel the little alien's homesickness like a kick to the stomach. I want to point east, toward the Rocky Mountains, and find a way to build something out of the stuff in Lila's garage that will let me go home.

By the time I'm finally allowed to climb the two flights of stairs to the bedroom that is not mine, I'm exhausted. It feels like I've had all my muscles held tight for hours and they ache. My head hurts, throbbing like there's a backlog of tears dammed up behind my eyes.

I pull out my box of lost kids and sit with it in my lap, cross-legged on the bed. I take my scissors out of my ballerina box and find the milk cartons I managed to carry back from the community center. I've already cleaned them. I just need to finish my ritual so I can finally sleep.

I start with Seth Delgado. He was fifteen when he went missing, three years ago. He's not even really a kid anymore. His hair is thick and dark, his eyes wide set. Like most of the kids in my box, his picture is a school portrait. Ninth or tenth grade, I think.

He went missing from Detroit. He is five foot ten and weighs 155 pounds. He looks athletic in the picture. Strong. If he couldn't get away from whoever took him, what chance did any kid have?

I'm about halfway done cutting out his picture when there's a knock on one of the windows in my room. It startles me, but when I look up, I see Jay Jay waving at me from the balcony.

I finish cutting out the picture, then go to open the door. "You scared me."

"Sorry. I saw the light come on. Finally."

"You were watching?"

He makes a face and shrugs one shoulder. "Sounds creepier than it is. I think. Want to come out?"

I look over my shoulder into the bedroom and decide that I'll be able to leave the milk cartons for a little while.

It's nice out. Warmer than it would be in Denver after the sun's gone down. It smells good, too. I can smell the salt water. Jay Jay leans against the balcony railing, his long legs out in front of him, crossed at the ankles. He came over in his bare feet, wearing shorts and a T-shirt.

"So," I say. "You know Lila."

"Kind of, I guess. Like I said, she's friends with my aunt Lucy."

"Your mom's sister?"

He nods. "She lives in Portland now. Went there for college."

"My dad just married Lila." I wince. He already knows that.

We just stand there for a few minutes. He finally says, "Your parents are divorced?"

I shake my head and take a breath. I always have to steel myself before I say this out loud. "My mom died last year."

"Oh." He gives me the look. Pity, mixed with a little dose of *I'm glad it's not me.* And something I haven't seen yet, but I'm sure I will again: he's embarrassed for me because my dad has married such a young woman so soon after my mom's death. I know what's coming next. It always comes. "I'm sorry."

Like it was his fault. Why do I have to forgive everyone else when it's my mom who died? "It's okay."

"Must be hard, though," he says. "I barely see my mom, and I can't imagine if she died."

I sit on the ground with my back to the wall, facing Jay Jay, and hug my knees. "How come you don't see her?"

He sits, too, with his back against the balcony wall. "My grandma says she's a wild child. She had me when she was in the tenth grade."

My parents were twenty-eight when I was born. His mom was only three years older than I am now when he was born. "Wow."

He shrugs. "She tried. For a while."

"Where is she now?"

"Last I heard, she was in Las Vegas. My grandma doesn't think she's with my dad anymore. She says drugs matter more to both of them than anything or anyone else."

The nicest thing I can do, I decide, is change the subject. "So why do you guys need to win the foosball tournament so bad?"

"It's a thousand bucks."

So they keep telling me. That's a lot of money. But Jay Jay lives in a mansion. His grandma has a *maid*. "It's just the money?"

It's not. I can see it in his face, even in the dark. He's looking at me with his different-colored eyes, like he's trying to decide whether or not he can trust me. I try to look like someone who can keep a secret.

If he tells me, it will mean that we really are friends. Not just maybe-maybe.

"You know those kids you collect?" he asks. "You think they have families who are looking for them?"

"Yeah, of course."

"Good families?"

I look harder at him, trying to figure out what he's getting at. "I mean, probably."

"Some kids . . ." He drums his fingers against his knees. "I mean, sometimes, it's better not to be found."

"How is it better?"

"I mean, not every kid was kidnapped or something. Right? Some of them, maybe . . ."

"Ran away?"

He shakes his head. "Escaped."

"Escaped . . . what are you talking about?"

"We really need you to help us win that tournament, okay? If you play with us, I think we have a chance." He leans his head back against the wall. "I didn't think we did before."

"Then why were you doing it?"

He looks at me again. "We have to do something."

"You're so confusing."

"Just—you're going to be there tomorrow, right? We're meeting at the clubhouse at nine."

"Don't you guys ever sleep in? It's summer."

"So you'll be there?"

"Yeah," I say. "But I still don't understand—"

He stands up and shoves his hands in his pockets. "We better get some sleep then. Night."

And just like that, my maybe friend is gone.

※　※　※

I'm exhausted. Not because it's late, but because I feel empty. Like someone has stuck a huge straw in me and sucked me dry.

But I have a ritual, and just like I can't leave a milk cooler without a new kid or turning over every carton, I can't skip this.

I trim the other two kids I collected today. I pull out my entire stack of cards—fifty-five now, which is a very satisfying number—and set them on the bed, leaning against my thigh. I take the top card from the pile and look at Christine Adams.

I whisper her stats out loud.

Four years old when she was taken from Topeka, Kansas, in

1978. Blond. Green eyes. Thirty-eight inches tall and forty-three pounds. She's eleven now.

After I've said every single thing I know about her out loud, I spend ten seconds staring at her picture, focusing as hard as I can on her face. I try to burn into my memory the shape of her eyes, the width of her nose, the way her chin has a small dip in the center.

I've done this so many times that I've developed a kind of inner timer. When the ten seconds is up, I put her card in the box and move on to the next.

Each card gets the same ten seconds. I have this ritual down to a science.

EIGHT

The next morning, I take a shower in the bathroom on the second floor.

It's filled with Dad's familiar things—the same shampoo he's always used. The old-fashioned shaving soap mug with a brush he swirls around in it, and then over his cheeks. His bathrobe hangs on the back of the door.

And it's filled with Lila's things, too. Her bathrobe, silky pink with flowers, hangs next to Dad's. Shampoo that smells like coconuts. Lotions and makeup that I've never seen before. Her crimping iron is on the sink.

It's like being half in the real world and half in some alternate universe where Mom's stuff—which Dad only put away a few months ago—has been replaced.

Once I'm in the shower I have a choice between Dad's shampoo and Lila's. His smells like Old Spice, but I use it anyway.

✳ ✳ ✳

"Good morning," Lila says when I come downstairs wearing a pair of cutoff jeans and a Broncos T-shirt. I have my damp hair in a braid and my backpack hooked over one shoulder. It's empty except for a sweatshirt in the bottom to cushion whatever milk cartons I find myself bringing home today.

I make myself a bowl of Cheerios, because they're already sitting on the table. There's a half-gallon carton of milk there, too, and I try to be casual when I turn it around. I see two girls I don't have. Laurel and Becca. The carton's still half full of milk.

"Is it okay if I have a glass of milk?"

"You don't have to ask," she says.

"Oh." I hesitate for a minute, because I'm not sure where the glasses are.

Lila opens a cupboard and hands me a little jelly jar with Mickey Mouse on it. She holds it in front of her face and says "Good morning, Tessa Hart" in a squeaky Mickey Mouse voice.

She's trying. I can see that, but I don't want to.

I have Dad in my head, too, asking me to help make it easier for her to deal with me.

"Did Dad already go to school?" I ask.

She hands me the glass. "He's getting his classroom set up."

"He said I could go back to the community center today. He said it was okay."

"I know." Lila smiles at me, but her face looks pinched. Like maybe she doesn't feel well.

"So it's okay?"

"Just call at lunchtime, okay?" She reaches into her pocket and pulls out a slip of paper she's written a phone number on. "Please, Tessa."

"I will." I want to leave now. Get my bike and go until the streetlights are on and Dad is back. But she really does look a little green. "Are you okay?"

She inhales through her nose. "Oh yeah. I'm fine. Just need to lie back down for a while, I think. Your dad took your bike out of the garage before he left."

I hesitate. I don't want to say what I know I should. But I do anyway. "Do you want me to stay?"

She shakes her head, and I'm relieved. I've made the effort. That's all I can do. I take my bowl and glass to the sink and run water in them. And then I realize it's still only eight o'clock, and I'm not sure what else to do.

An hour sitting in the kitchen with Lila will feel like a year.

"I'm grocery shopping today," Lila says. I think about the stock in the garage. She probably doesn't actually need to shop for a year. "Is there anything I can get for you?"

"The other guys bring snacks," I say.

Lila reaches for a big binder sitting on the table, and I see that it's filled to overflowing with cut-out coupons. "Perfect."

I don't want to show up in the clubhouse empty-handed, so I make myself ask, "Is there anything I can take for snacks today?"

Lila doesn't look up from her coupons. "There're apples in the fridge. And cheese sticks."

I shove five green apples and a handful of string cheese in my backpack and get out as fast as I can.

✳   ✳   ✳

I'm so anxious to leave the house that I don't realize until I'm standing on the little square of lawn that I don't actually have a plan for the morning.

I don't know if I should get my bike now, or go meet the boys in the clubhouse, or maybe knock on Jay Jay's door.

I walk around the corner to the front of his house.

It's like something I've only ever seen on television or read about in fairy tales. I can imagine Snow White or Sleeping Beauty locked in an attic bedroom by an evil stepmother.

Or a cranky grandmother.

The house is three stories, the same as Lila's, but it takes up half a block and is much taller. It has towers and spires and windows that are all divided into diamond-shaped panes.

There's a weeping willow tree in front that I wish I could crawl under to see what it's like inside those branches that reach all the way to the grass.

I could live in there, I think, with the birds and the squirrels. At least for the summer, until it gets cold. Does it even get cold in California? Maybe it doesn't. Maybe I really could move into a weeping willow tree permanently.

I stand there, lost in a daydream about sneaking some of Lila's garage hoard under the branches of the tree. It could be my own secret garden. The branches are so long and thick, no one would see me under there unless they came looking for me.

I look up at the house and think about Jay Jay there alone with his grandmother, like a couple of marbles rolling around in one of those empty industrial-size coffee cans Mom used to store my Legos in.

The front door is massive, at least twice as tall as I am, and there is no way I'm knocking on it. Maybe someday, when I know Jay Jay better, but not this morning.

Instead I walk toward the bluff. There are already people jogging and walking their dogs on the grass above the beach, and mothers with their small children setting up on the sand for the morning.

When I'm halfway down the stairs, I turn and look through the risers and see them there. All four boys are huddled toward the back of the clubhouse.

Pretty much no part of my life feels quite right. I don't belong in Los Angeles. I wouldn't belong in Denver anymore either, without Dad, no matter what kind of daydreams I might have.

I miss everything and everyone, and it makes me feel like I'm not heavy enough to stay on the ground.

But I get a boost of confidence when I hear their voices. They're waiting for me, I think. Maybe it's just because I know how to play foosball, but it's something. It helps, like it's poked a tiny hole in my homesickness, relieving the pressure a little.

I come all the way down and turn the corner to join them. "Hey, guys."

Oscar raises a hand toward me and says, "Shut her up."

I blink and take a step back. The tiny new bubble of belonging bursts. Jay Jay's head pops up from the back of the group, and he waves me over. "Don't be a jerk, O."

"This isn't her business," Oscar says before I can move—either to come closer or to leave. "We don't even know her."

Something has happened. Jay Jay, Oscar, and Petey all stand around Marvel. Like they're protecting him.

I stay where I am. "What's wrong?"

"Go home, Tessa," Petey says. His voice cracks on the word *home*.

"No." Marvel's small voice sounds calmer and stronger than his brother's. "We need her."

I am rooted in my spot. I don't want to butt in where I'm not wanted. I don't want to leave.

I finally just ask again, "What's wrong?"

Jay Jay walks toward me. I look at his green eye and then his blue eye and wrap my arms around myself. He takes my elbow and pulls me back out of the clubhouse, into the sun. It's a little like coming out of a cave, and I find myself blinking at the people, half surprised to find that they're so close.

"They had a bad night," Jay Jay says, his voice low.

"Who did?" I look back at the stairs, at the boys under it.

"Petey and Marv." Jay Jay exhales slowly. "Mostly Marvel."

I'm missing something and I know it, but I don't know what it is. I can't figure it out. "What kind of a bad night?"

Jay Jay seems to make some kind of a decision. "Their mom, okay? When she drinks, she does things. And she gets mean."

"Mean."

"Especially to Marv."

"She's *mean* to Marvel?" I hear myself just parroting back what Jay Jay says to me, but I can't seem to stop. "Mean to *Marvel*?"

"Tessa," Jay Jay says sharply. "She does stuff to him, okay. Bad stuff."

119

Bad stuff. My imagination is strong enough and has had enough experience imagining bad stuff happening to the kids in my shoebox to make me yank my arm away and take a step back. "Well—you have to tell someone."

"We can't."

I want to understand, but I really don't. "Why not? If their mom is . . . if she's *hurting* him."

"We've tried." I turn back to the stairs. Petey stands there with his hands shoved into the pockets of his Levi's.

"Is Marvel okay?" Jay Jay asks quietly.

"No. He's not okay." Petey's voice, his face—his whole body—is stiff.

"You told someone?" I put a hand over my mouth as soon as the words escape me. Jay Jay and Petey both look at me like I'm an idiot. At least I manage to keep my next question inside my head. *Then why is it still happening?*

"Yeah. We told someone, okay?" Petey shakes his head. "We told our dad."

"Well, why doesn't he do something?" Yep. The nosy questions just keep rolling off my tongue like I have some kind of verbal diarrhea.

And the second I ask that question, I know the answer.

I can see it in the way Petey's chin lifts and in the hollow sadness in his pale eyes.

His dad knows and he hasn't done anything to protect Marvel. It doesn't matter *why* he doesn't do something. What matters is that he doesn't. He hasn't.

I think about how upset I've been because Mom died. Because

Dad married Lila, and there's a baby coming, and we had to move away from Denver.

I think about how I've never even been spanked before.

"He did something," Petey says. "He left. Without us."

"That's why you need the money," I say. "So he can take you and Marvel away."

Jay Jay shakes his head, and Petey says, "We need the money so *I* can take Marvel away."

"You're going to run away?"

Petey takes a step away from me and turns back toward the clubhouse where Oscar is still with Marvel. "Damn it."

"I won't tell." I say that without really thinking it through. Because maybe I should tell. Dad would do something. He's a teacher. He *has* to do something.

"You can't," Petey says, an edge of panic in his voice, and I know there are still things that he hasn't told me. Like how his mom reacted to his dad leaving.

"I won't." This time, right or wrong, I mean the promise.

Marvel and Oscar come out from the clubhouse, and Marvel looks a little pale, but I don't see any marks or bruises on him. No one tells me exactly what happened the night before, so I still don't know just what *bad stuff* means, and I don't ask.

The three older boys rally around the smaller one, keeping him between them like they can protect him now from what happened the night before.

We make our way up the stairs to the street.

"You're going to practice with us, right?" Marvel asks me. "The first day of the tournament is tomorrow."

"Sure," I say. "Of course."

"Do you need Olivia's bike again?" Oscar's voice sounds like the words are too big for his throat.

I shake my head. "My dad fixed mine."

"Okay," Oscar says, drawing the word out. *Ooh-kaay.*

While the boys go to Jay Jay's house to get their bikes, I walk around to get mine, glad that none of them came with me. I don't know if the garage door is open, and I still don't want them to see Lila's stuff.

Dad has set my bike on the driveway and the garage is locked again, keeping Lila's stash safe. What would he do if Lila was mean to me the way Petey and Marvel's mom is mean?

If she was, and I told him, would he believe me?

Would he make excuses, because she's his brand-new, pregnant wife and I'm his daughter who carries around a shoebox full of missing kids cut from the backs of milk cartons?

A deep shudder runs up my spine, and I roll my bike down to the sidewalk before I can think on that any harder.

❊　❊　❊

Jessica isn't at the desk this morning. Another girl sits in her place. She's Jessica's age, probably in high school. Her name tag says *Jennifer.*

Jennifer's looking up at a teenage boy in a Greater Los Angeles Community Center T-shirt. His name tag says *Marcus.* Neither of them is paying attention to us at all.

Marvel runs ahead of us into the game room. The bike ride seems to have helped. He's his old self again, as far as I can tell.

If I hadn't seen what I saw in the clubhouse this morning, I wouldn't have any idea that something wasn't right with him. Except that since I do know, I can see him favoring his right side. Just enough for me to notice.

He's so small. Watching him jog toward the game room, so he can slap his hand on the foosball table and save it for us, I see how delicate his bones are.

He jumps in the air and brings his hand down on the rim of the good foosball table and yells, "Next game!" even though the only other kids in the room are two girls his age who are setting up house under the Ping-Pong table. They're building furniture out of wooden blocks for a pair of baby dolls.

Oscar rolls his eyes. "Good thing you screamed, Marv. I'm sure they heard you at their houses."

"It's all right," Jay Jay says, winking at Marvel. "Maybe they'll stay home then."

"Ha!" Oscar takes his place. "Like that's going to happen."

"Could," Marvel says.

"No." Petey takes his place next to Oscar. "It couldn't. Let's play."

* * *

Jay Jay, Oscar, and Petey are good. They've been playing together for a long time. I can tell without being told. They have a groove, like Megan and I used to.

Marvel stands at one end of the table and shouts directions.

Don't spin! You're not allowed to spin, O!

You always go that way, Petey. You should mix it up.

We're in our own groove an hour later when a hand slaps the rim table between Jay Jay and me. And an unfamiliar voice calls out in my ear, "Next game."

I look over my shoulder, and Oscar slams a shot past my defense. The boy behind me shrugs and goes back to his friends.

Marvel tugs on my arm and says, "Pay attention!"

I turn back to the game. Jay Jay and I hold Oscar and Petey off for a few more plays, then they score again and it's over. The four boys waiting for our table are the same kids from the day before. Ricky and Aaron and the twins whose names I can't remember.

"Threesies?" one of the twins asks.

"Yeah, sure," Jay Jay answers.

We do the same thing they did: stand back, pretending like we don't care, but watching their game pretty intensely. They're good—but I think maybe not as good as we are. If we only had to beat them, I'd feel pretty confident.

"What's threesies?" I ask.

"They'll play three games, then we will," Oscar says.

Even though there isn't anyone else waiting, Marvel goes to slap the table for the next round of "threesies." One of the boys goes for a save at the same moment and drives an elbow into Marvel's rib cage.

Marvel stumbles back and makes a sound I've never heard a person make before. Something between a whimper and a terrified squeal.

Something like the sound a dog makes if you accidentally step on its tail.

He stumbles back, and his brother is there. I don't even see Petey move, but he puts an arm around Marvel and glares at the boy with the wayward elbow. "Jeez, Ricky. Watch it."

Ricky looks our age but isn't much bigger than Marvel. He doesn't look away from his game, but he does offer up an apology. "Hey, sorry, Marv."

Petey mutters something under his breath, and my eyes fly back to the other boys, but they're too caught up in their game to notice.

"I'm okay," Marvel says. When Petey doesn't back off, he pulls away from him and says, "I'm fine. Let's just play on the other table."

Even though we'd played on the second table the day before, no one makes a move toward it today until Marvel reaches into the pocket and pulls out the ball Jessica gave him. I still don't quite understand the superstition regarding that table, but if it gives us extra practice time, what difference does it make?

"It's a good thing you're part of our crew now," Jay Jay says to me as we take our places. He tips his chin toward the tall boy with glasses standing next to Ricky. "Aaron knows our moves too well."

"Why isn't he a Loser anymore?" I ask.

"Playing in the tournament was his idea, but he decided if we won, he wanted to keep his share." Jay Jay takes the offense position, same as Megan always did. "So he put together a new team."

He points out each of the other boys.

The redhead is Ricky Levine. He's a real jerk. Not a friend-jerk like Oscar, I guess.

The twins, both of them about my height with dark buzz cuts and identical round faces, are Matt and Luke Kim. They look a little older than us. Maybe ninth graders, I think.

All of them are bent over their players, grunting as they play.

"They're pretty good," I say.

"Yeah."

"I think we're better."

Jay Jay's face breaks into a smile. Marvel drops the ball on the forbidden table, the Losers' table, and we start our practice.

I'm having so much fun that for a while, I don't even think about the cards in their box in the room I'll have to share with Lila's baby.

Or about calling Lila so I won't get in trouble.

Or about how Marvel's mom is mean to him.

Or the fact that at ten thirty, it'll be snack time and I'll have to face the milk cooler again.

I forget about all those things, right up until Jennifer sticks her head into the game room and says, "Snack time, guys."

I exhale slowly.

I want Jay Jay to remember yesterday and somehow know that I could really use a friend here. For a few seconds, I imagine him putting a hand on my arm, telling me everything will be okay, then helping me turn the cartons over until I find one I don't already have.

Preferably quickly.

But snack time isn't traumatic for him. Or anyone else.

I wish I could just skip it. I'm not even hungry, and if I were, I have a backpack full of today's divided-up snacks. But those cartons are there, with kids staring off the back of them, whether I look for one that's new to me or not.

I really am a mess.

Dragging my feet means that I'm behind Jay Jay, Oscar, Petey, and Marvel in line. And because they were finishing their game, the other foosball team—Aaron's team—is behind me.

Today's snack is a packet of cheese crackers. I have one last moment of hope that maybe milk isn't an everyday thing. Maybe crackers are served with a juice box.

But no.

I watch every kid in line ahead of me pick up a carton of milk without even looking at it. I try to will just one other kid to flip their carton over and at least *look* at the picture on the back.

None do.

The guy handing out the cheese crackers puts a bag in my hand, and I move forward like I'm on a conveyer belt, toward the big silver milk cooler.

The first carton I pick up is an eight-year-old girl named Abby. I know her well. In fact, if I want to, I can recite every bit of information about her that it's possible to get from the back of a milk carton.

I put Abby back, and Ricky crowds a little closer, waiting for me to get out of the way so he can go about his snack business.

I pick up another carton and see another face I instantly recognize. I've done this before. I know how it will go. I tuck my crackers under my arm and start turning over cartons as quickly as I can, using both hands. Ricky lets me get away with three sets before he starts to grumble.

"What are you doing?" He takes Abby from where I put her. I want to scream at him to at least *look* at her.

I just stay quiet and frantically turn each carton over. I'm methodical about it. Working from one end of the cooler and turning over every single container, then putting it back when I see a kid I already know.

Ricky says, "For real. They're all the same."

"No, they're not," I say quietly. Out of the corner of my eye I see my friends moving away with their snacks.

Tears build up behind my eyes. I want to stop. I want to not be *this* girl.

"Loser," one of the twins, either Matt or Luke, says. Great. "Get out of the way!"

He pushes against me with his hip and I stumble sideways.

The kid passing out the snacks says, "Hey, come on. Just get your milk and move on."

Does he really think I would stand here flipping over milk cartons if I had a *choice*?

"I can't," I whisper.

"She's touching every single carton!" a girl says. She's a little taller than me and much skinnier. All bones and joints and a cloud of brown curls. She's looking at me like I'm some kind of sludge stuck on the bottom of her shoe.

"I'm sorry," I murmur, but I go back to where I left off, turning over two more cartons.

"Just take one," the guy handing out the crackers says.

God, I want to. Please let me just walk away. I tense up, trying, but I can't do it. What if the next carton has a kid on it that I don't already have?

"Jay Jay, your girlfriend is a total freak!" That comes from somewhere behind me, and my cheeks burn.

"She's not Jay Jay's girl. I think she's Oscar's."

The skinny girl with the hair laughs.

I want to die.

There are at least fifty kids in the room, and just the one teenage boy handing out cheese crackers. I know without waiting to see what will happen that he'll try to manage me instead of them.

"Hey!" he calls out. "Watch your mouths."

Okay, so that surprises me. But then he puts a hand on my elbow and says under his breath, "Just take a carton, okay?"

Please, God, just let me take a carton. Yesterday I went home with *three*. Today I can't find one.

Before I can answer, Marvel is beside me. He starts to turn over cartons, showing them to me. Petey and Jay Jay are slower, but not by much.

Oscar stays by the door.

The second carton Petey turns over has a little boy on it that I've never seen. I grab the carton and whisper, "Thank you."

To Petey. To Jay Jay and Marvel. To Oscar who stayed over by the door, watching. To God. Whatever.

We eat snack in the game room, sitting along the wall behind the Losers' table. By the time I've finished my cheese crackers and milk, I feel better.

Now I need to check in with Lila.

The idea of calling her is weighing on me, and I figure I might as well get it over with.

"Marvel, can you play the next game?" I ask.

Oscar looks up sharply. "We need to practice."

"I just need to check in with my . . . Lila." I look at Aaron and his crew, leaning against the wall watching us, and lower my voice. "I won't be long."

Ricky stands up straighter, and Jay Jay waves him away. "Just hurry up," he says to me.

I carry my empty milk carton with me, thinking I can slip into the girls' bathroom after and at least rinse it out before I put it away. It would be nice not to lower myself from a mess to a mess who smells like sour milk.

The picture on the back of today's carton is of a seven-year-old boy named Stephen Davis. He's pale and has a sad look in his light eyes. Like maybe he knew that he was days or weeks or months away from being taken from his family.

Somewhere in Virginia, his parents, maybe his brothers and sisters, grandparents, aunts and uncles, have spent the last nine months wondering if he is still alive. They never stop thinking about him. I am sure of that. There's probably a closet full of unopened Christmas and birthday presents, stacks of missing child flyers on the dining room table, and his parents praying every night that he'll come home.

I dig in my pocket for the paper Lila gave me with her phone number written on it. My number, too, I guess. I should memorize it.

"Hey, Tessa." Jessica is at the desk now. She smiles at me, her finger holding her place on the page she's reading. That big textbook still.

"Can I use the phone? I need to check in."

"Sure." She pulls a big black rotary phone up to the counter with her free hand and goes back to reading.

After I dial, the phone rings three times. I have a moment of panic—what if Lila isn't home? She said she was shopping today. Maybe she's out adding diapers to her giant Pampers wall. If she doesn't answer when I call to check in, does it still count?

But before the fourth ring starts, Lila picks up. "Hello?"

I turn my back to Jessica and say, "It's me. Tessa."

I wince. Why do I have to sound like such a dork?

Lila hesitates, then says, "Having fun?"

"Sure. Just playing foosball."

"Okay."

We're both silent for a long time. Too long. Long enough that Jessica looks up at me again. I say, "Okay, well . . ."

"Thanks for calling," she says. Like I'm a stranger or something.

I hang up, and Jessica lifts her chin toward the game room behind me. Petey is standing in the doorway. He lifts his arms in a question. *Are you coming or what?*

What if all the practice in the world doesn't matter? What will Petey and Marvel do if they don't have that prize money?

What will they do if we win the thousand dollars?

On my way past the bulletin board, I pull one of the little phone-number flaps off the flyer the woman hung the day before. I don't know what a one-afternoon-a-week babysitting job pays, but it would be actual cash and not just a pipe dream.

NINE

Just like the day before, we ate our lunch at the picnic table. Everyone, including me, gave Marvel the most nutritious food from our collective stash.

After lunch, we have the whole afternoon to practice mostly uninterrupted. No one slaps their hand on the Losers' table.

"Won't last," Oscar says when we're on our way out to the bike rack at six. I'm the good kind of hungry. The kind that means anything you eat for dinner will be your new favorite food. "Pretty soon at least Aaron's new crew will want in on it."

"Yeah." Jay Jay spins the lock on his bike. "We'll see."

"Is the community center open every day?" I ask.

"Except Sunday." Marvel's face clouds over when he tells me that. "Sunday's the worst day."

I want to tell them about my idea for making some money over the summer. Real money that Petey and Marvel don't have to win. The words get stuck in my throat, though, like my jaw has rusted shut again.

Jay Jay puts an arm around Marvel and says, "We should camp out tomorrow night, after the tournament."

"Camp out?" I ask.

"No girls allowed," Oscar says as he walks his bike away from the rack.

"Tessa's not a girl. She's a Loser." Marvel looks up at his brother and asks, more quietly, "We can go, right?"

"Yeah," Petey says. "We'll figure it out."

"Where do you camp out?" I ask Jay Jay as we start to ride. "In your backyard?"

Megan and I used to do that in the summer, when it was warm. Our dads would pitch us a tent in her backyard or mine, and we'd pretend we were in the forest, scaring each other half to death with ghost stories.

"In the clubhouse," he says. "But that's a secret."

I ride beside him as he starts after the other boys. "Well, then, where does your grandma think you are?"

"In my bedroom. We sneak out." He looks at me, and I think maybe he's trying to decide if I'm brave enough. I want to be brave enough.

"Can I come?" I ask.

He nods and then pedals away. I pick up the pace, because if I fall too far behind, I'll never find my way home.

✳ ✳ ✳

Later that night, when my milk carton is clean and I've gone through my ritual, I sit on my bed and look at the little slip of paper I took from the babysitting flyer at the community center and an idea starts to take shape.

I'll tell the boys about it during the campout, after I see how the first day of the tournament goes.

There's a knock on my bedroom door, and I look up. "Yeah?"

"Lila made grilled cheese and tomato soup for dinner," Dad says. He looks tired, but in the good way, like how I feel hungry. "Okay."

He stays in the doorway looking at me. "How was your day?"

"It was pretty good," I say. And I mean it. "How was yours?"

"Not bad." He comes all the way into my room. He looks at the wallpaper, then the crib. This feels oddly formal. "Settling in okay?"

"I guess so. There's a foosball tournament that starts tomorrow. Jay Jay and Oscar and Petey want me to be on their team."

"Of course they do," he says. "You're a rock star."

"Yeah, right." Yesterday, he couldn't even remember if I played foosball or pinball with Megan. I make myself not look at my shoebox. It's sitting in its cubby in my headboard. Fifty-six cards inside now. I'm not a rock star. "I'm a Loser."

Dad sits beside me on the edge of my bed. "You're not a loser, Cookie."

When I said it, I was thinking about the boys and their foosball team name. And how nice it was to be part of something. But when it came out of my mouth, my voice cracked and now I'm on the verge of tears. "I am too. And not the good kind."

I pull the neck of my T-shirt up to wipe my wet cheeks.

"The good kind of loser?"

I nod, but he'll never understand. He looks at me for a minute, like he's trying to decide if he recognizes me.

"Tessa, I'm sorry about . . . everything." He swings a hand toward the crib. He looks at my shoebox, then back at me. "About all of this."

I shake my head. "It's okay."

"I miss your mom." His voice catches and nearly breaks my heart. "I miss her so much, Tessa. I wish she were here. I wish—"

I wrap my arms around his waist, ducking my head under his arm. The unbalance is painful. Like if I don't hold on tight enough, I'll slip off the planet.

"I'll try to do better," I finally say.

"Oh, baby." He tightens his arm around me. "You don't have to do anything better. I'm the one who . . ."

"Would it be easier if I did live with Gran?" He looks at me for a long moment, and I think that he's thinking about it. Wondering what it would be like if it was just him and Lila and the baby. A brand-new little family without the heavy weight of sadness constantly sitting on it. I try to stay calm, but I can't breathe.

I push away from him. "Then you wouldn't have to worry about me."

"You can't leave me." I've never seen my dad cry before, except for at Mom's funeral when he had to stand up in front of everyone and talk about her. He's not crying now, but his voice sounds strange. "Don't even think about it."

"I won't." How awful is it for Petey and Marvel to be so desperate to get away from their mom? It's been a long time since

I felt anything remotely close to lucky, but I feel it now, like a lightning bolt through me. "I won't go anywhere, I promise."

Dad laughs a little and pulls his glasses up to his forehead to wipe his eyes. Maybe I was wrong about him not crying. "We're going to pull through, you know."

"Yeah."

Dad tilts his head, and I try to look grown-up. "I know that I'm not doing this right. I don't think I've done anything right since Mom got sick."

I inhale, a little afraid that my lungs won't expand. "I wish I were more like her."

"What do you mean?"

A thought comes into my head and out of my mouth so fast that I don't have time to try to stop it. "I wish she were here, instead of me."

Dad grips my arms and pulls me to my feet in front of him. "Look at me."

I try. I really do. But it hurts to see his face. It hurts to know how much he misses Mom and to know that I'm just making things harder for him. I cross my arms over my chest and dig my fingers into my biceps.

He gives me a little shake, and I finally look at him. He looks back for a long minute. I wonder if he's wishing the same thing I am. He can't say it out loud. Ever. But I wonder if he thinks it.

"I wish," he finally says, and the sick feeling I've had in my stomach pretty much since I first heard of Lila twists. "Cookie, I wish that you could see yourself the way I see you."

I pull away from his grip on my arms.

"I know a lot of kids," he says. "A ton of them, and you are by far the coolest kid I've ever met."

"You have to say that. You're my dad."

"Your mom was only a few years older than you are when we met." He stays sitting on my bed, leaning forward a little toward me. "I was in the eleventh grade. Skinny kid, with glasses and acne, and I swear, Tessa, I knew, the moment she said hello to me, I knew I'd never meet anyone like her again in my whole life. But then—"

"But then you met Lila," I say.

"No. But then I met you."

"Did you have fun today?" Lila asks as she dips the tip of a grilled cheese triangle into tomato soup.

I decided before coming downstairs that I'd just leave out the awkward parts of the day, but I don't have to lie even a little bit when I say, "Yeah. I did."

"Good."

"There's a lady looking for a babysitter. Just on Thursday afternoons. I was thinking about calling her to see if I can do it."

Dad's eyebrows shoot up. "Is it a mom from the community center?"

But Lila talks over him. "Oh, that's a fantastic idea. I used to babysit all the time when I was your age."

Those kids probably still need a babysitter, I think, but don't say out loud. I just say, "Cool."

"I could introduce you to the families I used to sit for," she says.

I blink, because she made my point for me, and I don't let myself look at Dad. "Okay."

Dad asks, "Are you headed back for more foosball tomorrow?"

"Remember? The tournament starts tomorrow. I have to be there at ten."

"Right. Sounds fun," Dad says. "I'm glad you have something to keep you busy, actually. I'm going to have to work all summer, getting ready to start at my new school. I'm teaching political science. Did I tell you that? Seniors."

"No, you didn't."

"I'm so proud of you," Lila says to him.

It's been a long time, I realize, since I've seen him really smile. The way he smiles at Lila right now. I reach for the milk carton that's sitting on the table and turn it so the two girls on the back of it are facing me.

Laurel and Becca. A teenager and a little girl. Laurel is pretty, with long curly hair and a wide smile. Becca is six years old. She's missing a front tooth.

Dad puts a hand over mine and pulls it from the carton. "Thank you for remembering to check in with Lila today."

"You're welcome."

Lila takes a breath, then reaches for the carton, fills her glass with what's left of the milk, and hands it to me. "I found a good deal on your soap today."

My brain is having trouble processing the question of whether

I'll be able to use soap that smells like Mom if Lila bought it. I murmur, "Thank you."

I want to refuse the carton, but I can't. I want to get up and go to my room, but now that I have the empty carton, I can't do that either.

I absolutely do not want to start my ritual with Lila and Dad watching me. So, I just sit there with Laurel and Becca looking at me from their perch on the table.

"You're coming to the tournament, aren't you?" I ask my dad. "We need to leave about nine thirty."

"I wish I could. The department head called a meeting about that conference." Dad looks at Lila. "Can you take her?"

I can't make myself look at either of them. I'll start to cry if I do. Lila says, "Gordy."

No one says anything for a minute. Then Lila says, "Of course I can take her."

✳ ✳ ✳

Jay Jay said he saw my light go on the night before. I flip it on when I finally make it upstairs with the opened, flattened, clean milk carton, and I wonder if he'll come over again.

I set the carton on my desk and go to the door that leads to the balcony. If he can see my light, maybe I can see his, too.

I look toward the big house, and my eyes are drawn, instantly, to the only lit window. I don't know which one is his, but the window that has a light on is the tower room he told me belonged to his aunt Lucy. It's in a rounded turret directly across from my room.

The windows actually have many small diamond-shaped panes. It takes me a minute to realize that there is a message spelled out across some of them.

He's used something, maybe masking tape, to write out the word *Clubhouse* with one letter in each pane. Only they're backward for me. Still, the exclamation point makes my heart beat harder, which I suppose is the point.

It's dark out, and if I ask Dad if I can go to the beach now, he'll say no. If I tell him about Jay Jay's message, he'll probably insist on going next door to find out what's going on.

I pick up my milk carton and take it to my bed, so I can use my bird scissors to trim around Laurel and Becca while I think.

I follow through with my ritual—reciting their names, the information about them that the Center for Missing and Exploited Children has printed under their pictures.

As I'm finishing, I hear Dad and Lila moving around in the room below mine. They're getting ready for bed. I put my feet in my flip-flops and go back out onto the balcony before I can really think about them or about my mom or about anything at all.

As soon as I'm outside, I take a deep breath. And then I head down the long staircase to the lawn. I don't think about Dad coming up to say good night to me until I'm on the bluff.

I don't think he will. If he does, I'll be in trouble, but I'll cross that bridge when I get to it. I need to know why Jay Jay left that message for me in the window.

✳   ✳   ✳

"You saw it!" Jay Jay looks up from where he's sitting, on an upturned milk crate. The other boys are with him, all three of them. They've lit a fire in the broken shopping cart.

"Yeah," I say, suddenly shy. "I wasn't sure if it was for me. The letters were backward."

"Oh, shoot," Jay Jay says. "Sorry."

"Who else would it be for?" Oscar asks at the same time.

Jay Jay points to a milk crate across the fire from him, next to Marvel. I sit down and say, "So what's going on? I thought the campout was tomorrow."

"It is. We need to strategize," Jay Jay says.

"Tomorrow's mega important," Oscar adds.

The first round of the tournament. I wish that I'd had more time to practice with them. What if I choke and make them lose a spot in the finals?

"We only need to be in the top ten on the first day," Petey says. "I really think we can do this."

He seems surprised. Like maybe he didn't think so before I joined their crew. I want to be as good as they think I am. Good enough to make a difference. "Do you guys know the other kids?"

"Just Aaron's new crew," Jay Jay says. "The others are from other centers. We've never played them before."

"You can beat Aaron's crew, though?"

"We can," Oscar says. "Right. We can?"

"We have to." Marvel uses a straightened-out wire hanger to poke at the fire.

"Wait," I say. "You've never played against them?"

"We just practice," Jay Jay says.

Everyone gets quiet, and I squirm on my milk crate until I finally can't hold it in anymore. "What will you guys do with the money, if we win?"

Jay Jay, Oscar, and Petey all look up at me.

"*When* we win," Petey says. "We'll buy bus tickets and get the hell out of here."

"But where will you go?" No one says anything, and I can't help it. I need to know. "I mean, do you have somewhere to go?"

It's the boys' turn to squirm. Obviously, they've talked about this and they have things they don't want to say to me. But if I'm going to help them get money, I think I should know what they're going to do with it. Shouldn't I?

"Just tell her," Marvel says.

Oscar leans forward. "We don't have to tell her anything."

I am really getting tired of Oscar's attitude problem. "And I don't have to help you win."

"We have an uncle who lives in Michigan," Petey says. "We'll use the money to get to his house."

"You don't need a thousand dollars for that."

"We'll give our uncle the rest," Petey says. "So he'll let us stay."

I try to imagine my dad's brother, my uncle Henry who lives in Boise, not letting me stay with him if I told him that someone was abusing me. I try to imagine even worrying about that.

"But, I mean, you could get to him for a lot less, right?" I ask.

"What are you trying to say?" Jay Jay asks. "If you want to keep your share, then we'll just give Marvel back his spot."

I shake my head. "That's not what I'm saying."

"Then what?" Oscar asks. "This is just like Aaron all over again."

I reach into my back pocket and pull out the little slip of paper I'd taken from the babysitting flyer that afternoon. "This is what I'm talking about."

"What is it?"

"Some lady," I say. "She's looking for a babysitter on Thursday afternoons."

"You want to babysit instead of practicing next Thursday?" Jay Jay's voice is thick with disappointment, like he's wishing he'd never asked me to hang out with him and his friends in the first place, and my stomach falls to my knees.

"She'll probably pay me at least ten dollars a week," I say. "That's a hundred and twenty dollars by the time school starts again."

"Three months," Petey says.

"Well, just for that money. We could find other ways. All I'm saying is that we don't *have* to win the tournament. It would be awesome, but just in case."

"You don't think we can win?" Marvel asks.

"I don't even know the other teams or if they're good," I answer. "None of you do."

"What other ways?" Jay Jay asks.

I try to keep my breathing even, but my heart is pounding. "I don't . . . I don't know, what about all those people who I see jogging and walking their dogs in the morning? We could have a lemonade stand."

"A lemonade stand? Are you serious?" Oscar asks. "No one makes any money with a lemonade stand."

"We could," I say. "Seriously, there were so many people out there this morning. Lila does this coupon thing. I bet she could get us some Kool-Aid and plastic cups cheap."

Oscar rolls his eyes. "We need to practice, and she's talking about Kool-Aid."

Jay Jay looks at me across the fire. "We could mow lawns."

Oscar makes a noise, like he's disgusted.

"What about the tournament?" Petey asks.

"Of course we're doing the tournament." Jay Jay sits back again. "It can't hurt to have a backup plan."

"Just in case," I say.

"You'd really give us your babysitting money?" Petey asks.

I've been so caught up in having an idea that the boys might like, that I haven't really spent any time thinking about what it really means.

Would I give them money to run away with? What if I did and something terrible happened to them? Would it be my fault?

"She wouldn't," Oscar says when I wait too long.

No. He's wrong. I know it as soon as the words are out of his mouth. "Yes. I would."

"Why?" Marvel asks.

Because I saw you limp, I think. *Because I want you all to like me.* "Because I want to help."

Petey puts a marshmallow on the end of a hanger for Marvel. "Maybe it wouldn't be a bad idea."

"No," Oscar says. "We need her to practice with us."

"The community center is closed on Sundays," Jay Jay says

before I can respond. "We could try the lemonade stand idea on Sunday. See how it goes."

"Well, we're practicing next Thursday." Oscar crosses his arms over his chest, like he's waiting to see what I'll do.

"Marvel could practice with you for a couple of hours."

"No," Jay Jay says before Oscar can open his mouth. "We need you."

"Fine," I say.

Jay Jay sticks a marshmallow on his own hanger. "Good."

"I'll ask Lila about getting us the stuff to set up a lemonade stand Sunday." Oscar rolls his eyes, but Jay Jay nods and Petey just stares into the fire.

"We just need to make it to the finals," Oscar says. "That's what we should be focused on."

"We are," I say. "I am."

"Good."

"But—" All the boys look at me. I don't want it to be me, but someone has to ask. "Does your uncle know you're coming?"

Marvel looks up at Petey, and I wish I could suck the question back in. He doesn't know the answer. And I know, somehow, I know without being told, that Petey might have lied to me, but he won't lie to his brother. Just like my dad won't lie to me.

"Not yet," Petey says. "Not until we're on our way."

Not until they're away from their mom. There's more that I want to ask. Does their uncle know about what their mother does to Marvel? Does he know that after a bad night, his nephew limps around the community center? If he does know, why doesn't he come get them?

"Can't you just tell him about your mom?" I ask.

Petey inhales deeply. "If we tell him, he might say no."

I blink at that honest answer. "Well, then . . ."

"If we just show up, he might let us stay. At least long enough for me to make another plan."

"Won't your mom try to get you back?"

"Jeez," Oscar says. "Just shut up."

Jay Jay changes the subject. "How are we going to handle tomorrow?"

Only two of us can play at a time during the tournament. We'll have to choose starters for the first game. They've made such a big deal about me practicing with them and how much they need me that I expect someone to say that Jay Jay and I will play in the first game.

"Me and you first," Oscar says to Petey.

There isn't any non-jerk way to say *What do you mean I'm not playing in the first game?* Or to point out that I'm their best player. But more than that, Petey's too close to the problem. If I were him, I'd choke, and I think there's a good chance that will happen tomorrow.

I shake my head, and Oscar says, "What?"

"It should be me and Jay Jay."

"Full of yourself much?"

"She's right," Petey says.

"Seriously?" Oscar asks.

"Me and Tessa first, then," Jay Jay says, cutting Oscar off.

I exhale slowly. *Please, God, don't let me be the one who chokes.*

TEN

During the half-hour drive to the Boys and Girls Club, I hope Lila will pull in and drop me off. Instead, she parks her car and cuts the engine.

"What are you doing?" I ask.

"I know you're upset your dad can't be here."

"It's okay." I can't look at her. It's her fault he has to have a new job. It's her fault we're in California at all.

And it's also her fault that I have new friends and that I'm about to meet Andre Whittaker and play in a foosball tournament with Jay Jay and Oscar and Petey.

I want her to not make me think about this. Why can't she just drop me off and go home until I call for a ride?

"Mrs. Sampson is coming," she says. "She told me last night."

Jay Jay's grandmother will be in the stands? "Oh."

"I thought I'd keep her company." Lila shrugs one shoulder. "I needed to get out of the house. Is that okay with you?"

I don't want to be happy that I'll have someone there, cheering me on, even if it's just Lila. But the fact is that I am. And I'm surprised that she asked my permission. I get out of the car without saying anything except, "Okay."

The indoor basketball gym at the Boys and Girls Club has been set up with a dozen foosball tables. The wooden stands on both sides of the court have been pulled out and are filled with parents and grandparents waiting to watch their kids play.

A hard knot of panic rattles around my sour stomach as I scan the crowd looking for the boys. It settles some when I see Oscar standing with his mom, who is standing next to a tall, very thin older woman. Jay Jay is on the other side of her, with Petey and Marvel.

The older woman spots Lila and waves her over.

"There's Mrs. Sampson," Lila says. She doesn't move yet, though. "Are you ready to kick some foosball butt?"

"Uh . . . yeah." Actually, I am. I start toward the boys, and Lila comes with me.

Marvel runs to me as soon as he sees me.

"What—?" He's wearing something that looks like a cross between pajamas and a Halloween costume. A one-piece suit that covers every inch of him in soft brown fur. He pulls up a hood that has bear ears and a black nose. "What are you wearing?"

"I'm the mascot." He stands on his toes and points toward the back of the stadium. "Do you see him?"

I follow his finger. "Who?"

"Andre Whittaker."

And then I do see him. He's wearing his uniform, and I see him shake a boy's hand and say a few words. That kid moves away and another steps forward. A line has formed behind him, waiting to shake Whittaker's hand.

Marvel takes my hand and pulls me toward the soccer player. I look back over my shoulder at Lila, and she waves at me.

"Petey, come on!" Marv calls out, and the other boys join us as we get in the back of the line.

A team from the Long Beach YMCA sends two girls to play against us in the first round. *So much for throwing off the other team with a girl player*, I think. The girls wear matching barrettes braided through with purple ribbons that hold back their hair behind their right ears. One of the girls has a waterfall of dark-blond hair falling down the left side of her face, and she reminds me so much of Megan that for a minute I can't breathe.

Somehow everyone but me knows that the next thing to do is reach across the table and shake hands with our opponents.

"Good luck," I say to the girl who takes my hand when I finally offer it and squeezes a little too hard. I try to pull mine back, but she holds on even tighter.

"You too," she says in a way that clearly means *You're going to need it*.

"Each game will play until one team scores ten," Andre Whittaker says into a microphone.

Ten. We've only ever practiced to five. Megan and Denny and I always played to five. I look at Jay Jay, but he doesn't seem worried.

A man and a woman hold huge television cameras. The man

focuses on Andre Whittaker. The woman scans the players. I duck my head when she swings our way, suddenly shy about being filmed.

A girl in a *Third Annual Los Angeles Foosball-Palooza* T-shirt stands near our table with a ball in her hand. She spins it around her palm and waits until Andre says, "Play ball!"

The ball drops, and the girl across from Jay Jay gets control immediately. Before I can react, she slams the ball past our offense and into our goal. Five seconds in and we're already losing.

The girls high-five each other, and Jay Jay looks at me.

You didn't stop it either. But I don't say that. I feel Oscar glaring at my back.

Our table's tender takes the ball again and drops it. This time, I'm more alert. Like someone's poured ice water over my head. Jay Jay gets control of the ball. He lifts an eyebrow as the girls bounce on their toes and keep their eyes on the table.

He passes the ball back to me, and I tap it across to the far side and back up to him. When the girls are settled in to block a shot there, he suddenly shoots it across to his offense on the other side of the table and scores.

I breathe easier with the score tied up. For the next several minutes, our game stays that way. I block two attempts by the girls. Jay Jay doesn't even try to shoot against them. I feel like I'm playing our side by myself, and I can't take a minute to look up at him to see what's going on.

"Get your head in the game, Jay!" Oscar calls out from behind us.

"I'm trying," he says under his breath as he crashes his front line of offense forward, trying to block a shot that makes it back to me.

I tap the ball back up to him, all the way against the side nearest us. He finally seems to get himself together and shoots through the girls' defense and scores again.

I have about ten seconds to be relieved that we're ahead before the girls score two in a row, one right after the other. Jay Jay misses the block both times and worrying about what's going on with him divides my attention too much.

Petey, Marvel, and Oscar behind us aren't making it easier. I hear them groan when the score goes 2–3.

Petey says, "Are you kidding me?"

We should have played against Aaron's team last week. All of Jay Jay's practice has been against his friends. He is completely thrown off by these girls and their more aggressive style.

And we should have practiced playing to ten. A 2–3 score should be a half-over game, but it's not now. We've barely started.

A boy at the table next to ours calls, "Time out!" and I look at Jay Jay and do the same thing.

"Time out! Time out!"

The girls lift their hands in the air, then huddle together while the tender picks the ball out of the middle of the table.

"I'm sorry," Jay Jay says. "I don't know what's wrong with me."

"Let's switch. Let me take the offense."

"You're killing it in defense, though. What if I can't—"

"You can."

"I've never played defense."

"Yes, you have. You did the first time I saw you play."

Jay Jay's eyebrows shoot up. "With Marvel!"

"Just block the goal."

The girl holding the ball says, "Time."

Jay Jay and I switch places, and I wrap my hands around the offensive controls. I breathe out slowly, trying to stay calm. The girl across from me, the one who looks like Megan, snorts a little burst of laughter and I look up at her.

We need eight more goals, and we need to block at least six from them. For now, though, I focus on getting one more past their keeper, to tie the game up again.

Megan sometimes could sneak one past Denny when he got too sure of himself. When he was positive he had us beat, he'd lose enough of his focus to drop his guard, and Megan could send a ball right through, dead center. No tricks or anything.

I win the drop, and the girl across from me moves her front line back toward her. For a split second there's an opening, just like Megan sometimes had against Denny. Right up the middle, when the other team is sure I'm going to try to sneak it in from the side and even more sure they can block it.

I shoot as hard as I can and hear the girl across from me say a swear word under her breath. The ball slips right past their defense and into the pocket.

We're tied up again. My heart pounds. The score is 3–3. Jay Jay blocks a shot and passes the ball back up to me. They do the same when I shoot. Back and forth. Back and forth.

And then I sink another one, and we're ahead. 3–4.

"One more," Oscar says behind me.

Thanks. I can count. But obviously you can't. I need six more. Six.

For the next couple of plays, I'm just chasing behind the girls, running myself ragged like sometimes happens in a real soccer game when the other team is better. Even though I'm standing in one spot, I'm breathing hard, like I've been running the field from the goal to the half over and over.

Somehow, we stay even with them, though. They score, then we do. Every time they get the ball past Jay Jay, I get a jolt of adrenaline and somehow manage to power it past their keeper.

The only problem is that if we keep up this pattern, they'll win. Our last score brings it to 9–9, and I'm so anxious I can't breathe.

"One more," Oscar says again. At least he caught up with reality.

And suddenly it's over. I score again, and the game stops. The girl across from me spins her front line in frustration, and the tender says, "Don't do that. Shake hands."

I reach across the table and the girl hesitates, but finally takes my hand. "Good game," I say.

"Good game."

When Jay Jay is done shaking hands with the player across from him, he turns to look at me and my face breaks into a smile. He gives me a double high five and then Marvel is there, with his arms around my waist, jumping like a jackrabbit.

"You did it," Oscar says. "I can't believe you pulled that off."

"Thanks a lot," I say.

"Not you." He shoves Jay Jay's shoulder. "What happened to you?"

"I don't know."

"You're too used to playing against each other," I say.

Jay Jay looks up, like he's checking for spies. There are still a handful of games going. "Maybe Tessa should play in the next game. She won this one."

"It's ours," Oscar says.

"She's right, though. I was thrown off by playing someone other than you guys. If I'd been playing with any of you, we'd have lost."

"We won't lose." Oscar is unmovable. And the last of the games are finishing.

Each team's name is written on a giant chalkboard, matching teams up for the second round of the day. Every team plays six times, getting a point for a win. The ten teams with the highest scores move on to play next Friday in the finals.

Next Friday, the teams that are left standing will play a standard elimination final series until there is just one winner who will take the $1,000 prize.

I look around at the other teams. Some of the kids look much older than we are. Some are dressed in matching uniforms. Marvel is looking up at me with the hood of his bear costume falling over his eyes, and I think, *Our lemonade stand better work*.

Petey and Oscar are creamed by a team of high school boys. Creamed. They don't score at all and the whole thing's over before any of the other games have even properly gotten started. It's painful to watch.

"Come on," Jay Jay keeps saying. *"Come on,* what are you doing?"

Petey and Oscar have the same problem Jay Jay did. They're totally thrown off by plays they aren't used to, and there is no time to recover. The goals come fast and furious. No time to talk to each other, since neither calls for a time-out. No time to strategize. The shots just keep coming. Petey does his best and manages to block some of them, but not enough. Oscar never even comes close to scoring.

If this were real soccer, they'd need stretchers to take them off the field.

I look up at the stands and find Lila. She has a hand over her mouth. Oscar's mother and Jay Jay's grandmother are leaning close to each other. All three of them look like they're watching a train wreck.

"This is so stupid." Petey kicks at the bleachers with the toe of his sneaker. "What were we thinking? We're never going to win."

"Don't say that." Jay Jay puts his hand on Petey's shoulder before the boy can kick again.

"Why not? It's true. We really are losers," Oscar says.

"Who's best in the goal?" I ask.

They all turn to me.

Marvel pushes his hood off his head. He looks overheated to me, and I wonder if he's wearing shorts under all that fur. He says, "You are."

I shake my head. "Besides me. Who is best?"

Jay Jay tips his head. "Petey is."

I try to work through a strategy that is only just starting to take shape. "No, that won't work. Between you and Oscar, who's best?"

"What do you mean it won't work?" Petey asks.

"You already play defense. We need to shake it up." They all look at me and I wrap my arms around my chest, but I don't back down. "Jay Jay and I did better when we switched."

"Oscar's better than I am," Jay Jay says.

I was afraid of that. I look at Oscar, and he's glaring at me. He doesn't trust me. I'm right, though. We'll do better if we play positions we're not so used to. The boys need to stop expecting the other players to play how they want them to.

"So who's playing offense?" he asks.

"Petey," I say.

"No." Petey shakes his head. "It has to be you, Tessa."

"What?" The referee blows his whistle, and the sound makes me jump.

Petey lifts his eyebrows and tips his head toward the table. The other team is already there. "You're better than I am."

"Are you in or what?" Oscar asks.

My hands and feet tingle and my ears are ringing, like all the blood in my body has rushed to my head. I look up at the stands again, and Lila waves at me.

You can do this, Soldier. I hear Mom's voice in my head, and I have to look away from Lila. I wish Dad were here. Or Gran. Or Megan and Denny.

I rub my fingertips against my palms and then rub my palms hard against my hips, bouncing on my toes. Oscar takes his place beside me and pulls the keeper back and forth, like he's testing the rod.

Our tender bounces the ball on his palm once, twice, and then when the ref blows the whistle, he drops it in the center of the table.

I lose the drop, and Oscar groans. The boy across from me gives a little whoop as he passes the ball back to his defense. The defender sends it flying through my front line to Oscar, who blocks the shot.

He keeps the ball for a minute, passing it just up from the keeper to the defensive line. When I look back at him, he says, "Ready?"

I take a breath. *You can do this, Soldier.* "Ready."

He passes the ball to me. We've given the other side a chance to regroup, and they're ready, too. The boy on defense bounces on his toes and pulls his keeper and his defensive line back and forth, like two saws moving in opposite directions.

"One."

The boy looks up at me.

"Two."

He crouches down and readies himself. Like I'm counting down for him, letting him know when I'm going to shoot. He expects me to say three and then go. So when I shoot on two, sending the ball hard toward the far-left corner of the goal, he's not ready.

That won't work again, but it worked once. The ball goes in.

* * *

My strategy for the game, combined with the good luck of playing against a team that wasn't as good as the first two we were up against, works.

Oscar and I win.

The guy at the chalkboard writes "The Losers" in the ninth slot for the finals. For three more games, we manage to stay right there. Ninth. Only one of the top-ten teams is worse than us, but we do it, even with an iffy first game and a terrible second game.

"You were amazing," Lila says to me when we're in her car, as she struggles to get the seat belt around her huge belly. "I wish your dad had been here to see that."

"Me too," I say.

"He wanted to be. You know that, don't you?"

I hardly need Lila to tell me what my dad wants. A few minutes ago, I was flying high. My new friends were hugging me. For the first time in a long time I felt like I belonged somewhere. That good feeling takes a hard shift now and anger floods me.

My jaw rusts shut again. If I speak, I'll say something awful. But it's not like the something awful is bursting to come out, either. I don't want to hurt Lila's feelings.

I can't make myself say anything at all.

But on the way home, Lila asks me if I want to go grocery shopping with her, and I remember something that makes me finally pry open my mouth. "We want to have a lemonade stand."

She looks at me, then back to the road. "You and Jay Jay?"

"And the other guys, too. By the beach."

Lila makes a little sound and nods her head in approval. "That's a great idea. The bluff is always packed."

"Will you help me buy the stuff?" I ask.

"Can you reach my binder, behind you?" I turn in my seat and pull the heavy binder into my lap with a grunt. It must weigh ten pounds. "See the divider that says 'beverages'?"

I flip the book open and run my finger past coupons for frozen orange juice and canned soda and chocolate milk powder.

"I think I have some coupons for Flavor Aid," Lila says.

I find them, at least a dozen clipped from the Sunday paper. Flavor Aid, fifteen for a dollar. Where does she get so many? "I see them."

Lila pulls into the grocery store parking lot without asking me again if I want to go with her. After she pulls herself out of the little car, she stops for a minute and puts a hand on her lower back. I watch her, a little worried I'm going to have to go get help, but then the pain on her face passes and she goes to get a cart someone's left two parking spots down.

I prop her giant coupon binder in the baby seat and wonder what she'll do when she has to put a baby there. "When will Dad be home?"

"He should be there when we get home." She stops walking. "What's your favorite? We should have your favorite dinner tonight. To celebrate."

"Oh." Her excitement about the Losers making it to the finals is embarrassing for some reason. For a minute, I can't even remember what I like to eat. I finally spit out, "Spaghetti?"

She smiles. "Perfect. With meatballs?"

I haven't had spaghetti, with or without meatballs, since the last time my mom made it for me.

Lila watches me struggle to figure out what to say, then just smiles and says, "That's good then." She goes back to pushing her cart toward the store.

She's as uncomfortable as I am. That hits me hard. It hadn't occurred to me before. I follow behind her and test the idea of her making spaghetti for me and decide that it should be okay. It won't be just like Mom's anyway. Mom put grape jelly in her meatballs.

Dad sits at the kitchen table and listens to Lila tell him all about the tournament. I want to tell him myself, but she's gushing and hearing her talk about me has tied my tongue into knots. My face feels beet red.

Dad reaches over and chucks my chin gently with his fist. "I guess you really are a foosball champion. I wish I could have been there."

"I wish you could have been, too," Lila says. "She was amazing, Gordy."

Dad twirls spaghetti around his fork. He's not really eating, and I wonder if he's remembering, like I did, that the last time we had this dinner Mom made it for us.

I was right at least; it doesn't taste like hers at all. Still, I wish I'd said pork chops or meatloaf.

"Can you come next week?" I ask Dad. "For the finals."

Dad looks at me, and my stomach sinks. I know what's coming, just from the way he exhales slowly. "It's fine," I say, before he can tell me that he won't be there.

"I can be there Friday," he says. There's a *but*. I feel it in the air. "But my flight to Portland is in the morning."

"How long will you be gone?" I ask.

"Just until Tuesday."

Lila asks the next question before I can. "Do you have to go?"

He looks miserable and doesn't say anything. I wait, but when he still just sits there, I say, "Do you have to, Dad?"

If he says he has to, then I'll believe him. I'm not one hundred percent sure about whether or not he'll lie to Lila, but he doesn't lie to me.

He finally sighs and sits back in his seat. "It's not mandatory exactly. But I've been strongly advised that I should be there."

I should be upset. He's leaving me alone with Lila for—

"How long will you be gone again?"

"I'll be home Tuesday morning. Early," he says.

For three days, practically as soon as we've set foot in California. I barely even know Lila. But it helps that he told the truth. He still doesn't lie to me. "It's okay."

"Are you sure?" he asks. And he means it. I think he'll stay, if I tell him I need him to. He'll believe me, the way I believe him.

"I think so."

"Lila will be here," he says. Then he looks at her. "Won't you?"

She's not as easy to forgive as I am. Her arms are crossed tightly around her, above her belly. "Of course I will be."

"Thank you," he says. To both of us. I look from one of them to the other, and it suddenly hits me. They don't have any sort of silent back and forth. Mom and Dad used to have whole conversations just looking at each other. He would have been able to smooth things over with Mom without saying a word.

"I'm going to have a lemonade stand on Sunday," I say, to change the subject. "With my friends."

"Oh yeah?" Dad says.

"Lila bought the stuff for us today."

"Starting your empire, huh?" He's talking to me, but he's still looking at Lila.

I want to tell him. About Petey and Marvel and their mom. About why the tournament matters so much. If we actually do win, I'm going to have to figure out some way to explain why I don't have my part of the money.

I'm meeting the boys at the clubhouse at midnight. Late enough that all the grown-ups will assume we're in bed for the night and will probably be in bed themselves and not get up to check on us before morning.

Not telling Dad that I'm going to camp out at the clubhouse isn't the same as lying, I tell myself again. If it were, then he'd lied to me every time he was with Lila before the day he told me he was marrying her. And I can't let myself believe that.

Jay Jay's bringing an extra sleeping bag for me. We'll all leave notes that we went to the beach early, so no one misses us in the morning, if they check.

The boys have done this before. *It never fails,* Oscar said.

Dad has left the house without saying goodbye to me practically every day since we got to California, so I doubt he'll even know I left.

And if he does find out?

I don't let myself think about that right now. There's no way I'm missing this campout.

✵ ✵ ✵

I wait until Dad and Lila are on the sofa watching a movie on her box-top VCR before I go upstairs to check Lucy's turret window for any messages.

Nothing.

"Hey."

"Oh my God." I nearly come out of my skin, my heart beating so hard it actually pushes me back a step. Jay Jay stands on the balcony in the dark, to the left of the door. I was so focused on the window at his house that I didn't even see him or that the door was open. "You scared me!"

"Sorry." He's got a blue sleeping bag in his arms, rolled up tight. "I just wanted to bring this by. And make sure you're still coming tonight."

"I am." I take the sleeping bag and put it on my bed, next to my shoebox that is sitting out.

Jay Jay's blue and green eyes take it in. "Those things are really important to you, huh?"

"They aren't things," I say. "They're people."

"I meant the cards."

"I know." I don't want to talk about it.

"I wonder if they'll put Petey and Marvel on a milk carton? If we pull this off."

I hadn't thought about that. Jay Jay saying it out loud makes me uncomfortable. I sit on the edge of my bed and watch him as he moves to inspect the weird doll wallpaper.

"We could tell my dad," I say. "He'd help them. Teachers have to."

Jay Jay turns to me. "You promised."

"I know. But running away is—"

"It isn't really running away. They just need to get to their uncle. Everything will be okay after that."

"How do you know?"

He leans against the changing table. "Their mom didn't used to be like this. She's sick or something."

"Sick how?"

"Something happened to her, before Marvel was born. Petey doesn't know what, exactly. He was only five. But something. She started drinking, and whatever it is, she takes it out on Marv."

"We really should tell my dad," I say again.

"They've told before, and it only made things worse. There isn't anything your dad can do."

"He can call the police."

Jay Jay shakes his head. "That happened once."

"Someone called the police?"

"Marv's kindergarten teacher caught him stealing food out of the other kids' lunch boxes."

"What happened?"

Jay Jay takes a deep breath. "They went to separate foster homes. Their mom got them back, but it took six months."

"Seriously?"

"I guess things got better for a while. Then they got worse. Much worse. This year has been bad."

Jay Jay leans over to my bed and picks up the box of missing kids. He takes the first card out and holds it toward me, so I can see Christine Adams's face. She has full cheeks and an easy smile. Her stats come to me. "She's about Marv's age."

"I know that. But—"

"Petey's smart. He's smarter than any of us. If they get to Michigan and their uncle won't help them, they can get help there. Away from their mom. It's not like they're really running away." He puts Christine Adams back and flips through the cards, barely glancing at each face. He finally looks up at me. "They have to at least try. Petey has to try. You promised not to tell."

I did promise. I'm not sure what I'll do if something terrible happens because I keep Petey and Marvel's secret, but I did promise.

"They'll be separated again," Jay Jay says quietly. "And it will be worse this time, especially for Marvel."

If I did tell, would Dad even think about what happens *after* he makes his report? I love my dad, but he didn't think very hard about making me leave Denver and our house and my school and soccer team and friends.

Adults think they know everything, but sometimes they miss the most important parts. "I won't tell."

ELEVEN

The rest of the evening goes so slow, I think I might lose my mind. Every time I think it must be nearly midnight, I look up and only ten minutes have passed.

"You're driving me crazy with your fidgeting, Tessa," Dad says. "Why don't we pull out the Scrabble board?"

"No!" That comes out too harsh, and both Dad and Lila look at me. Dang it. "I mean . . . can I just go to bed?"

"Are you okay?" Dad asks.

I should say that I have a headache. Or maybe that I'm just tired. But I'm not either one, and I don't want to lie. Between the campout and not telling about Petey and Marvel, I'm already skirting too close to that line. "I'm fine. I just want to read the book Lila gave me."

Dad looks at Lila, and it happens. That little bit of talking without saying anything. *Is it all right with you? I don't care if you don't.* I pluck the words out of the air, as if they're really flying past.

"Okay, Cookie." But I'm already halfway to the stairs.

Upstairs, I lie on my bed and pull out *Petals on the Wind*. It helps me forget about the look between Dad and Lila.

Lila is not my mom. She never will be. I don't want to like her. I don't even want to know her. But she isn't so bad. And Dad wasn't doing very well, if I'm totally honest with myself, when we were in Denver.

Maybe he needs someone to talk to without talking.

* * *

"Lila bought us the lemonade stuff," I say. "It cost five bucks. After we pay her that back, the rest is ours."

The fire was already going in the grocery cart when I got to the clubhouse at midnight. All the boys were sitting around it. Someone brought hot dogs and Marv had one on an unbent hanger, sizzling.

"I'll be surprised if we can make enough to even pay her back," Oscar says. "This is such a stupid waste of time."

"Don't be a jerk, O," Jay Jay and Petey both say.

"There are a ton of people on the beach in the morning." I sit on one of the milk crates. "It could work."

Oscar shakes his head. "Waste of time."

"It's worth a try anyway." But I'm starting to wonder if this is a good idea after all. These boys are going to hate me if we spend a whole Sunday trying to have a lemonade stand and we can't even earn enough to pay back Lila.

"I called Greyhound today," Jay Jay says, and we all turn toward him. "A one-way ticket to Detroit costs thirty-nine fifty. It's three days, so some money for food. We need to make, say, a hundred dollars."

"We need to give some to our uncle." Petey shakes his head

when Marvel offers him a hot dog. "We have to win that tournament."

"But in case we don't," Jay Jay says. "Just a plan B. We need about a hundred dollars."

"And you think a lemonade stand will do that?" Oscar looks at me. "Or babysitting on Thursday night?"

"It's better than nothing," I say.

Oscar lifts his eyebrows and opens his mouth, but Jay Jay cuts him off. "Let's talk about the tournament."

Oscar says, "We sucked."

"Some of us sucked worse than others." Jay Jay reaches for the package of hot dogs and sticks one on a hanger. "But we made it through to the finals."

"Barely." Petey takes the hanger when Jay Jay offers it.

"But we did," I say. I've had an idea brewing all afternoon, and I try to put it into words. "How well do you know Aaron's crew?"

"I told you, Aaron was a Loser. Ricky goes to our school, but we don't hang out with him. I don't know Matt and Luke at all." Jay Jay asks the others, "Do you?"

Oscar and Petey both shake their heads.

"They go to Eisenhower," Jay Jay says. "Doesn't matter anyway. Aaron's new crew didn't make it to the finals."

"Will they practice with us?"

All three boys look at me like I've lost my mind.

"We don't want them to," Oscar answers. "They're the enemy."

"Oscar's right," Jay Jay says when I turn to him.

"Well, we need to find *someone* to play against this week

in practice." They all give me blank looks. Weren't they at the same tournament I was today? "You guys are too used to playing against each other."

"And you think the answer is to play against Aaron's crew, which couldn't even make it to the finals," Oscar asks.

"Well, I just got here. I don't know any other teams."

"Neither do we," Jay Jay says.

Everyone is quiet then, and I finally reach for a hot dog myself. I know I'm right, but I can't make them listen. Petey eats his burned hot dog right off the end of his hanger, the same way that Marvel had.

Between the fire and the hot dogs and the ocean, the clubhouse smells wonderful. Marvel has opened his sleeping bag and is lying on it, near Petey.

"I'll call Aaron this morning," Petey says. "After our mom goes to work."

Oscar adds another stick to the fire. "This is so stupid."

Jay Jay sighs. "Don't be a—"

Oscar turns on Jay Jay. "I'm not a jerk, okay?"

Jay Jay holds his hands up. "I'm sorry."

"I just don't want to miss practice time because some girl we barely even know says so."

"We'll still practice," I say. "We'll just practice better."

"Great." Oscar unrolls his sleeping bag onto the sand and lies down with his head on his backpack. "I'm still not a jerk."

My cheeks burn. "I know you're not."

He grunts once, but his body relaxes some.

"So what about Aaron's new crew?" Jay Jay asks.

"I said I'd ask, okay?" Petey's voice sounds tight and angry. "Obviously we have to do something different next weekend."

✻ ✻ ✻

Oscar's watch buzzes at six in the morning. The fire has gone out, and I'm inside the sleeping bag that Jay Jay lent me.

The alarm woke me from a dream about Denver. Nothing in particular, just Denver. My nose is filled with the scent of pine and snow, instead of burned-out campfire and ocean.

It takes a minute for me to get fully back to California. I sit up and rub my hand over my eyes.

Jay Jay is already up, folding his sleeping bag. I don't see Petey and Marvel at all. Oscar seems to be sleeping through his own alarm. Jay Jay pushes Oscar's hip with his toes. "Come on, O. Get up."

I stand and stretch. I have to pee so bad it hurts. "So now what?"

"Sneak back to bed without waking up your dad," he says. "And meet us back here at nine. We're going to the community center to practice."

✻ ✻ ✻

I make it back into my room before seven, and the note I'd left on my pillow is still there. I look at the bed and realize way too late that I made a mistake. The note says that I woke up early and went to the beach, but my bed is made. Dad would never believe that I made my bed so early in the morning without anyone telling me I had to.

I pull the blankets down and get under them, wiggling

around a little to make the bed look slept in. It feels so good, lying on a soft mattress after a night on the sand that I stretch out and think another hour of sleep might not be such a bad thing.

Except I really do have to pee. I get out of bed and take the stairs down to the first floor. When I come out of the bathroom, Dad's in the kitchen making coffee.

When I see him, I feel a little guilty about sneaking out the night before. "Morning."

"Morning, Cookie."

He just keeps looking at me until I say, "Is everything okay?"

"Everything's fine. I just wanted to say goodbye before I head for the airport."

Portland. "Are you sure you have to go?"

He sets his coffee down on the counter. "I'll only be gone until Tuesday morning, and then I'll have some time to hang out with you. And I'll be at your tournament on Friday."

"Promise?"

"I promise." He leans over and kisses my forehead. "Be sure to help Lila, okay?"

"Help her with what?"

"With whatever she needs help with. She's not feeling very well."

I'm hungry, but it still feels weird to just take food from Lila's kitchen. "What do you mean?"

"She's fine," he says. "Her back's hurting, that's all."

"I really wish you didn't have to go."

"I'll call you tonight," he says.

He doesn't say that he wishes he didn't have to go, too.

Lila walks into the kitchen and stops, her eyes closing. "I wonder if the smell of coffee will ever stop making me feel like I want to die."

Dad pours the rest of his cup into the sink, then picks up the half-full pot and pours that out, too. "I'm sorry, honey. I'll get some at the airport."

"Ready?" Lila asks me. "We need to get on the road."

"Oh." I look at Dad. "Do you mind if I stay? The boys are practicing today."

"I'm not sure if I like the idea of you out without anyone here," he says.

"Mrs. Sampson will be home." I turn to Lila. "Please."

"I'll be back by ten," she says to my dad. "I think it'll be okay."

Dad reaches to brush my hair from my forehead. "You'll be safe?"

"I promise." I look at Lila. "I'll call at lunchtime to check in."

Dad smiles. "Okay then."

I go back upstairs. Another hour of sleep really does sound good. Maybe even two.

Before I leave the house, right at nine a.m. I pick up the kitchen phone and exhale slowly before dialing the number on the little slip of paper I pulled from Mrs. Norton's flyer.

The phone rings twice before it picks up, and a little kid's voice says, "Hello."

"Oh." I've built myself up to speak to an adult, and I'm suddenly not sure what to say. "Augie?"

"Yeah!" the kid says, like I've won *The Price Is Right*. "Who's that?"

"Um. Tessa. Is your mom—"

"August Norton, how many times do I have to tell you not to answer the phone?" I hear a little struggle, then Mrs. Norton speaks directly into the phone, "Norton residence."

"Um—" I force myself to take a breath and start again. "Hello, my name is Tessa Hart. I saw your flyer at the community center and—"

"Oh!" The phone goes silent for a second, and I imagine the nurse who reminded me of my mom holding the receiver to her chest. Then I hear her home in the background again before she goes on. "Oh, thank you so much for calling."

"You're welcome."

"What was your name again?"

"Tessa Hart. I just moved here with my dad. I've been playing foosball and I saw your flyer and—"

"How old are you?" she asks.

"Twelve."

Mrs. Norton goes quiet again, and I'm certain she's going to tell me that I'm too young. Or that she wants someone with references. Or maybe she'll let me down easy by telling me that she's already hired a sitter, even though I could tell by her reaction that it isn't true.

"Have you ever babysat before?" she asks.

I think about Petey and Marvel, and a little white lie comes flying out of me before I can stop it. "I've helped take care of my friend's brother. He's seven."

It's not enough. *I* wouldn't let me take care of a four-year-old.

"Are your parents okay with you watching my son on Thursday nights? I don't get off work until seven."

"My dad knows I'm calling," I say.

"I can pay you fifteen dollars a week," she says. "Since you'll have to fix Augie's supper."

That's five more than I guessed, and the only thing I can think of to say is "I make really good macaroni and cheese."

"I'm sure he'll love that," she says. "I'd like to meet you in person before Thursday. Could you and your mom or dad come by sometime this weekend?"

"Would tomorrow evening be okay?"

✳ ✳ ✳

Lila is curled on the sofa. She looks a little green around the edges, but she sits up straighter when I stop in front of her.

"Headed to practice? Your dad took your bike out for you."

"I am," I say. "But actually, I called that lady I told you about. The one who's looking for a babysitter on Thursdays. She wants me to come tomorrow at six to meet her. She wants to meet an . . . um . . . an adult, too."

I still can't say parent, but Lila doesn't seem to notice. "That should be okay. Did you get an address?"

I hand her the slip of paper with the phone number printed on one side, and an address scribbled in pencil on the other. She looks at it and says, "That's not far at all."

✳ ✳ ✳

There's a group of girls playing on the good table when we get to the community center. Aaron and Ricky are rallying the ball back and forth from keeper to keeper on the Losers' table.

"I don't know if we can teach you very much in one day," Ricky says. "But we figured we might as well try."

Oscar stands beside Ricky and stares at him until he walks around the table to take his place beside Aaron. Petey takes the defense beside Oscar.

Marvel acts as tender, dropping the ball so the play can start.

"I called that babysitting job," I say to Jay Jay when no one is paying attention to us. "I'm going to meet her tomorrow night, with Lila."

"Are you going to tell her that you can't start until next week?"

I look up at him. I don't want to lie. "I think she really needs someone this Thursday."

"Tessa."

"It's not until four. She's paying me fifteen dollars a week. Even if the lemonade stand doesn't work and we lose the tournament, there would be enough money in six weeks."

Jay Jay looks at me for a minute. The boys are getting into their game. Oscar slams his offensive line forward and blocks a pass. "I'll handle O."

TWELVE

When I take Lila's giant plastic pitcher over to Jay Jay's on Sunday morning so we can fill it up with ice from his grandma's freezer, it's the first time I've ever been inside his house.

His grandmother sits at the kitchen table, drinking tea out of a fancy cup with a matching saucer and working on a crossword puzzle in a folded-up newspaper. She looks at me over the rim of her reading glasses as I follow Jay Jay in.

Jay Jay takes the pitcher from me and leaves me standing in front of his grandmother while he goes to fill it.

"You're Lila's new girl, then?" She sets her paper down and turns more squarely toward me. She's wearing a white pantsuit with a pink blouse that matches her low-heeled pumps. She looks like she's ready to go to work.

She calls me Lila's new girl like maybe she thinks I'm at the house to wash the windows.

"I guess so," I say.

"She's not much older than you. The same age as my Lucy."

"Yes, ma'am."

"Lila O'Neil was a nice young lady before she moved to Colorado."

I'm surprised to find myself feeling defensive of Lila. Whatever it is that Mrs. Sampson is trying to say about her, and probably about my dad and me, too, I don't like very much. "She's Lila Hart now."

Her cheeks turn as pink as her blouse. "Yes, well. I suppose that's true."

"And I'm pretty sure she's still nice."

"Ready?" Jay Jay says before things can get any worse. He's holding the pitcher, filled with ice cubes.

"What are you doing with all that ice?" Mrs. Sampson asks. "You must have cleaned us out."

"There's plenty more, Grandma. We'll be back when we run out."

"Joshua Sampson." I guess she's not completely against calling him by his father's name after all.

"We're just having a lemonade stand," he says. "Across the street. I told you last night."

Maybe someone as rich as her doesn't want her grandson to be seen selling powdered lemonade across the street from her mansion. But she purses her lips and shakes her head, then picks up her newspaper again in one hand and her pen in the other.

She looks at me, though, before we leave. "You tell Lila that I expect to see that baby when it comes."

"Yes, ma'am," I say. I wonder, though, why she didn't tell Lila herself at the tournament on Friday.

* * *

Between the five of us, we lug gallon jugs of water, packets of pink lemonade Flavor Aid, a five-pound bag of sugar, and two sleeves of Styrofoam cups down into the clubhouse.

Oscar peers at the little paper envelope of drink powder and says, "One cup of sugar. Did anyone bring a measuring cup?"

Petey and Marv are up on the bluff, setting up a card table with a sheet Lila gave me to use as a tablecloth.

Jay Jay and I look at each other and groan. One of us will have to go back up and across the street.

"Rock, Paper, Scissors?" he asks, holding his hands out, one fist resting in the other palm.

"Forget it," Oscar says as he lifts the sugar bag and starts to tip it into the ice pitcher. "I'll just eyeball it."

The sugar coats the ice cubes. Oscar twists his mouth to the side, thinking, then tears open three envelopes of Flavor Aid and pours them in, too.

"Three?" I ask.

Jay Jay opens one of the gallons of water and pours it in. The pitcher holds about half of it.

"We don't have a spoon, either?" Oscar sighs. "You guys suck."

Jay Jay puts the jug down and picks up an unbent hanger that probably has the residue of a hundred burned marshmallows and hot dogs on the end of it. He sticks it right into the pitcher and stirs. I manage not to say *Ew* out loud.

Oscar pours some of the lemonade into a Styrofoam cup and takes a sip, then hands it to Jay Jay. He sips, too, then hands it to me.

The Flavor Aid is sweet enough to make my teeth hurt, and extra tart. There's at least one too many packets of powdered mix in there.

Oscar picks up the pitcher and heads for the stairs. "No one's going to buy it anyway."

I pick up the gallon of water so I can dilute the lemonade, just in case he's wrong.

✳ ✳ ✳

Marvel's made a sign with crayons and construction paper that says: *Lemonade 25¢*.

There are just as many people on the bluff today as there has been every day since I got to California. It's at least eighty degrees outside, even before ten in the morning, and I think some of them must be thirsty.

Jay Jay puts the full pitcher on the table and Petey sets out cups.

And we wait.

And we wait.

And we wait.

The ice starts to melt. People go by with their dogs and their roller skates and their jogging shorts. They look at us, but they don't stop.

This is going to bomb. We aren't going to make any money, and I'm going to owe Lila five bucks. Worst of all, I made the boys waste a Sunday sitting here on the bluff with a pitcher of lemonade that no one wants. Including us.

"Great idea, Tessa," Oscar says after an hour has passed.

I want Jay Jay or maybe Petey to tell him not to be a jerk, but they don't. "It's not my fault."

"She's right," Jay Jay finally says, after a too-long pause. "It was worth a try. I guess."

Oscar starts to walk away, back toward the stairs down to the beach.

"Where're you going?" Petey calls out.

"I'm hungry." He starts down the stairs toward the clubhouse, where our backpacks are. I have little packets of applesauce and juice boxes in mine.

Petey goes after him and looks back at Jay Jay, who shrugs before leaving, too. I stand there until they've disappeared and then turn back to the lemonade stand.

Marvel lifts both of his shoulders as I walk toward him. It's time to pack it in. I wonder what the boys usually do on Sundays. And whether they'll include me today. Before I can ask, though, a woman holding two little kids by the hands stops in front of the table.

"Well aren't you adorable," she says to Marvel. "You're out here all by yourself?"

Marv smiles up at her and doesn't skip a beat. "My big sister is with me."

The woman looks at me, and her smile widens. Her children are a blond little boy and an older girl with curly brown hair. Like Marv and me. They tug at her arms, trying to get to the beach. She lets go of the girl, who is maybe five or six years old, and says, "We'll take two."

Marvel does look *adorable*, struggling with a pitcher that's half his size, pouring two glasses of pink lemonade right to the rim. The woman hands him a dollar and waves off the change before taking the Styrofoam cups and giving them to her kids.

Another woman has stopped behind her; she's got a big yellow dog on a leash. She hands me a dollar bill.

"We're saving up money to buy a dog." Oh, Marv's good. "We want a wiener dog."

He stands on his toes and pours her a cup of lemonade. She smiles at him and when I try to give her three quarters change, she shakes her head and tells us to keep it.

It's like everyone on the bluff this morning was just waiting for someone else to be first to buy our lemonade. I look back toward the stairs after the fourth customer, with three more in line, and see Oscar, Jay Jay, and Petey standing there, staring at us with their mouths hanging open.

Jay Jay says something to Oscar, and they both go back downstairs. Petey starts to walk toward us. I'm a little afraid that he'll break whatever spell has given us so many customers, but it doesn't seem to make a difference.

The other boys come back with a gallon of water and the bag of sugar. Jay Jay's holding the rest of the packets of Flavor Aid in one hand.

✳ ✳ ✳

"Ho-ly crap," Jay Jay says. "I can't believe it."

At some point, before we ran out of Styrofoam cups, shoving quarters and dollar bills into our pockets stopped working. Oscar brought up Marvel's empty backpack from the clubhouse.

Now there's a pile of bills and coins inside.

"All right," Oscar says. "The lemonade stand wasn't a *terrible* idea."

Petey reaches in for a handful of dollar bills and starts straightening them out. It takes fifteen minutes to get everything sorted. Marvel puts the quarters into little stacks of four and Oscar counts the dollar bills.

Then Petey counts them, because it seems impossible that we've earned one hundred and fifty-four dollars.

"Ho-ly crap," I say under my breath.

It's more than what Petey and Marvel need for the tickets to Michigan. My heart tightens as I realize that even without winning the tournament, they have enough money to run away.

Maybe I shouldn't have come up with the whole lemonade stand idea after all. Chances are pretty good we won't win the tournament. If I'd left well enough alone, I wouldn't have to think about what to do when my friends get on a Greyhound bus. Alone.

Petey hands me five one-dollar bills to give to Lila, then five more to pay back the five dollars in quarters she gave us to make change. "Tell her thank you, okay?"

I shove the money into my pocket. "Okay."

I wait for there to be some discussion about what to do with the rest of the money, but it doesn't happen. Marvel digs an old lunch box out of the cooler and puts the cash into it, then puts the whole thing into his backpack.

✳ ✳ ✳

At six o'clock, Lila pulls her little purple car into the parking lot of an apartment complex about halfway between the house and the community center. I'll be able to ride my bike here if this works out.

The building doesn't have an elevator, and Mrs. Norton lives on the third floor. Lila takes the stairs slowly, stopping at the landings for what seems like a really long time.

"Are you okay?" I ask.

"I'm fine. Just kind of worn out."

When we finally make it to apartment number 352, I wait a minute while Lila catches her breath and smooths her hand over her hair. When she nods at me, I knock.

There's a bang about halfway down the door, and the knob rattles. I hear Mrs. Norton on the inside saying, "Augie, how many times do I have to tell you to let me answer the door?"

Too late, I realize that I'm not sure I'm ready to look at a woman who reminds me so much of my mother while I'm standing next to Lila. If Mrs. Norton's in her scrubs and her light-brown hair is pulled back in a braid the way it was when I first saw her . . . my throat starts to ache with tears that haven't even threatened to fall yet.

The door opens, and Mrs. Norton grabs Augie by the arm before he can dart out into the hall. "I swear," she says, "he's on hyperdrive tonight."

She's wearing a yellow sundress and her hair is down, held back in the front with a scarf. The ache in my throat lets go, and I take a deep breath.

Lila holds a hand out to Mrs. Norton. "I'm Lila Hart."

"Julia Norton." Mrs. Norton looks like she really wishes it was Lila who'd called about the flyer. But she looks at me and says, "You must be Tessa."

I nod. "Yes, ma'am."

Mrs. Norton looks back at Lila. "Are you Tessa's sister? I don't suppose you babysit."

"Tessa's my stepdaughter," Lila says without choking the way I do, whenever I have to define who Lila is to me. "She'll be great with your son."

Mrs. Norton steps back, pulling Augie with her so we can come inside. Her apartment looks a little bit like a tornado has landed on it. Legos and toy cars and the pieces of a Monopoly game are everywhere.

Under Augie's mess, though, it's a nice apartment.

"My regular sitter can't cover my whole shift on Thursdays," she says. "I need someone to keep an eye on Augie, fix him supper, get him ready for bed. Do you think you can handle that?"

Augie looks at me from where his mother is holding him, against her side. I offer him a smile, and he sticks his tongue out at me. "I think so."

"We're less than two miles away," Lila says. "I can be here in five minutes if they need me."

Mrs. Norton visibly relaxes and releases Augie so he can go to his toys. She has nurse hands, I notice. Dry and rough from so much washing, just like my mom.

"He's a handful," Mrs. Norton says. "His dad moved to Sacramento last year, and he's still trying to adjust."

Lila and Mrs. Norton start talking about babies, and I slide off the sofa to my knees near Augie. He's building something with his Legos that looks like a cross between a building and a robot.

"Can I play?" I ask him.

He gives me a sideways glance, then pushes a pile of little bricks toward me.

What would Mrs. Norton say, I wonder, if she found out that her fifteen dollars a week is going into a runaway fund? When both women stand up a few minutes later, I have to look away. From my position on the floor, looking up at them, I see my mom in Mrs. Norton again, and when she spontaneously hugs Lila it twists my insides.

"I think this will be a nice little job for you," Lila says when we're in her car.

"Thank you for coming with me."

Lila doesn't reply or put the car into gear. When I look at her, I see her fingers are gripping the steering wheel so hard that her knuckles are white. "Do you think you could heat up some soup for dinner tonight? I'm really not feeling well."

I look back at the apartment building. "Should I get Mrs. Norton? She's a nurse."

Lila shakes her head and puts the car in reverse. "I just need to rest."

THIRTEEN

"Tessa?"

I look up from my bowl of chicken noodle soup. Lila is standing with her back to me with both hands on the edge of the kitchen sink. "What?"

"I need you to call your dad." Her voice sounds wrong. It takes me a minute, but I realize what it is. She's scared. Like she's seen a bear outside the kitchen window or something.

"What's wrong?"

"Please, Tessa."

And then I see it. There's a puddle of liquid on the linoleum under her feet. It looks like she's wet her pants. I put my spoon down and stand up. "I don't know the number."

"He's—" She leans into the sink and moans. Her belly seemed huge a few minutes ago, but suddenly I'm sure it isn't big enough. The baby isn't due until August and it's only the middle of June.

"Lila?"

She slowly straightens and turns to look at me. Her face has a grayish tint to it. "We'll have to call him from the hospital."

No. That can't be right. It's too early. "Should I call 9-1-1?"

She shakes her head. "I can drive."

I'm not even sure she can make it to the car. I *am* pretty sure that my dad wouldn't want me in a car with someone who looked about to pass out. "Are you sure that's a good idea?"

"I'll be—" I actually see her stomach tighten, and she leans forward, like someone's punched her in the gut.

"I'm calling 9-1-1."

Lila sits in the chair I stand up from. Her blond hair is pulled back in a ponytail and she's wearing a white T-shirt and a blue pair of maternity shorts that are soaked through. She doesn't seem any older than I am and for the first time, it really hits me how scared she must be.

She takes a breath and tries to say something. "I don't think . . ."

I wait for her to finish, but she doesn't. "I have to call someone."

Lila runs her hand over her stomach. "Maybe it's just something I ate or I have the flu or . . ."

She moans again, it sounds like something between a curse and a prayer. I look at the list of phone numbers taped near the phone. None of them look like they'd reach my dad.

"Oh my God." Her voice is hoarse. "I want my mom."

I want mine, too. Badly. "Do you want me to call her?"

"My parents are in Jamaica."

I forgot. "She might know what to do. Do you have their number?"

"They're on vacation." She sounds so sad. But she shakes herself and straightens. "My mom wouldn't be any use right now anyway."

My eyes land on the only number that looks even remotely useful to me. I pick up the phone and dial for a cab.

"Go get me some clean pants," Lila says after I hang up.

"I don't think anyone cares if . . ."

"Please."

I take off, sprinting up the stairs. I hesitate for a second at her bedroom door. I've never been in there. I've barely been able to make myself look at the closed door on my way to my room. Lila's next moan vibrates up the acoustic stairs, and I turn the knob.

The bed is rumpled and unmade. The room doesn't smell like Dad's old bedroom did. Dad's room still smelled like Mom. Like her soap and her shampoo and the perfume she wore when they went out. I'm glad this room doesn't smell like that.

I go to the tall dresser and close my eyes for a minute before opening the top drawer.

Underwear. I close the drawer again, hard enough to startle a note of music from a jewelry box sitting on top of the dresser.

It's pale pink with gold flowers painted around the edges and for a second, I can't take a breath. Lila has stolen my ballerina box. I'm too stunned even to be angry.

Does she think this is how she can make me stop collecting my milk-carton kids? I'm a little surprised to realize that I didn't even know my jewelry box was missing. I haven't actually opened the cubby where my box is . . . was . . . since the campout.

When I lift the lid, to make sure that my scissors are still in the box, a little ballerina pops up and I know as soon as I see her and the music starts playing that this isn't my box.

My ballerina wears a white skirt and is posed with one leg out behind her. This one has both feet on the ground and her skirt is baby blue. And the music is different.

Instead of a pair of bird scissors, Lila's box is full of plastic beads and clip-on earrings. Like a little girl's dress-up box.

I find Lila's maternity shorts folded in the third drawer down. I open the underwear drawer again and make myself take the top pair.

When I come back down into the kitchen, Lila is leaning on the sink, holding onto her stomach with one hand and keeping herself upright with the other.

"Do you want—" I hold her shorts and underwear out to her, but she cuts me off with a low moan. "Should I go get Mrs. Sampson?"

Lila slowly straightens herself, as if whatever was happening has passed.

"I'll go get her," I say. "I'll be right back."

Before I can go, though, there's a honk outside.

"It's okay," Lila says. Only I don't think she's talking to me. "It's okay. It's okay."

She does not sound okay, which makes me feel very, very not okay. I don't know what to do. She's supposed to be the grown-up here, but she's clutching underwear against her huge belly and I really want my dad.

"We can try to reach Gordon from the hospital," she says, maybe reading my mind. She takes a breath and starts walking toward the front door. I guess she's just going to carry her dry clothes. I grab my backpack from the counter and catch up with her. Before she opens the door, I take the clothes from her and shove them in. I take her purse from the hook by the door, too.

The cab driver is young. He looks barely older than Denny. He peers out at us and then gets out of the car and comes around to the passenger side.

"We're going to St. Joseph's," Lila says, only the word *Joseph's* is cut off when another wave of pain hits her. She clings to my arm and I stumble a little, but I manage to keep us both on our feet.

"Hey, lady," the guy says. "Maybe we better call an ambulance."

Lila shakes her head. For the first time since I've known her, she doesn't look beautiful. Her hair is a mess, her face is red and splotchy. She doesn't look ugly, really, just scared and ragged. Like a cat that's spent a couple of nights stuck in a tree.

"I'm not—" The driver looks honestly terrified. Before he can finish his sentence though, Lila has opened the back seat of his cab and pushed herself into it. "I don't think this is a good idea."

Lila ignores him all together. "Get in," she says to me.

I'm not sure whether to go around and get in next to her or sit in the front. I'm afraid that the driver is going to just stand there as long as I do, though, so I open the nearest door and climb in the shotgun seat.

Lila reaches an ice-cold hand between the seats and grips my fingers. She keeps a hold on me until the driver finally gives up and gets in the car, and she doesn't let go until he pulls into the emergency entrance at St. Joseph's hospital fifteen minutes later. Not even when another contraction makes her squeeze so tight, I feel my bones rub against each other.

Lila shoves a ten-dollar bill at the driver, and I think he must be so relieved to drop us off. I would be, if I were him. We're barely out of the cab before he takes off.

I look around, not quite sure what to do now. "Maybe I should . . ."

A nurse passes us, and I feel my knees go a little weak. Her light-brown hair is pulled back into a ponytail full of curls, just like my mom wore hers to work in Denver. She's built like my mother, compact. Small, but not too delicate.

"Wait!" I call out when the nurse starts to go into the emergency room ahead of us. "Please, wait."

She turns back to me and breaks the spell. Her face is nothing like my mother's, but I know her. "Mrs. Norton."

She looks at me, but her attention is drawn immediately to Lila. "Let's get you a wheelchair."

* * *

Mrs. Norton wheels Lila in a wheelchair into a room where she can wait for her doctor, and things are suddenly much calmer.

"I'll call Mrs. Sampson," Lila says. "Maybe . . . maybe she'll come pick you up. You can spend the night with Jay Jay."

It is too early for the baby to be born. That's the only thing that we know for sure.

Okay. And that we haven't been able to reach my dad yet. And Lila's parents are in Jamaica. They knew the baby was due in the next few weeks, but they went on their vacation anyway. I saw in Lila's face how much that hurt her.

I guess we know a lot. It all adds up to the fact that if Mrs.

Sampson comes to pick me up to spend the night at her house, Lila will be completely alone.

"I want to wait for Dad," I say.

"We can leave him a message at his hotel, but it might be late before he gets it."

He'd have to get a plane ticket to come home from Oregon. Lila doesn't say that he might not make it in time, but I know it anyway.

Lila's legs are so long, she has to bend them a little to keep her feet from hanging off the end of the bed. I can't leave her here alone.

I sit in the chair by the window, and she takes a breath and exhales, leaning back against her pillows. She's attached to wires and monitors, and her fear is like a lion in the room with us.

✳ ✳ ✳

I realize later, after Lila has left her message for Dad and after a nurse has brought me a tray with a turkey sandwich, cooked carrots, some yellow Jell-O with a tiny, hard dollop of whipped cream on top, and a pint of milk that I need to call Jay Jay.

I don't want to. I want my dad to somehow magically show up tonight, so I don't have to be the one keeping Lila from having a baby all by herself.

And so I can go to practice with the boys in the morning.

Except, I don't really want that either. I'm worried about Lila and the baby. It's like a hard lump in the center of my throat that I can't swallow down.

I don't think I'd leave, even if Dad were here.

What I really wish is that I could split myself in two. Stay with Lila, and hopefully soon my dad, and also not disappoint my friends. And while I'm at it, maybe a third version of myself can go back to Denver to hang out with Megan and plant flowers with Gran.

But I can't do that. And I need to let Jay Jay know I won't be there in the morning.

"Do you know Jay Jay's number?" I ask.

Lila has her hands on her belly, her fingers rubbing over the round globe of her baby. They stop when she looks at me. "Do you want Mrs. Sampson to come for you?"

I mean to say, *No. I'll stay here with you.* But for some reason the words stick. My jaw is rusty again. Maybe she doesn't want me to stay. Maybe it will be easier for her if Jay Jay's grandma takes me off her hands.

Maybe I don't belong here.

I finally unstick my jaw enough to ask, "Do you want me to ask her to?"

Lila takes a ragged breath. The kind that happens when you're trying not to cry. She shakes her head and says, "Please stay with me, Tessa."

I feel that lump in my throat let go. "I will, but I should let Jay Jay know I won't be able to practice tomorrow."

"I'm sorry," Lila says. "Maybe your dad will be here tonight and Mrs. Sampson can give you a ride in the morning."

He won't be. He hasn't even called yet. I pick up the phone and dial as Lila gives me the number. It rings twice, and a woman picks up. Oscar's mother, I think. "Sampson residence."

"Mrs. Montoya?" I ask.

The woman hesitates. "Yes. How can I help you?"

"This is Tessa Hart. I'm Oscar's friend. I've been playing foosball with him."

"Tessa, of course. Do you need to speak to Mr. Jay Jay?"

I nod, then realize she can't see me, and my cheeks burn. She can't see that either. "Yes, please."

She sets the phone down. I expect to hear her call for Jay Jay, but I don't hear a thing until the phone rattles again and his voice says, "Hello?"

"Hi," I say.

There's a moment, before I tell him what I've called for, when I'm still part of his crew. I'm still going to practice with the boys in the morning. None of them are mad at me.

"Tessa? What's up?"

I take a breath and just let it all out at once. "I'm at the hospital with Lila. She's having the baby early, and I can't come to the community center tomorrow morning. My dad's not even here."

There's silence for a few seconds, then, "Well, that sucks."

"I know. I'm sorry. I really am. Lila said I could go, but I just . . . I don't think I can leave her. We haven't been able to reach my dad yet and her parents are in Jamaica."

Another too-long moment of silence. "Yeah, of course you can't leave her alone."

"I really am sorry."

"Okay."

"Okay?"

"Yeah. Okay. I have to go."

"Well—" I don't know what to do. I thought he'd be angry or hate me or something. But this is even worse. It's like he doesn't care. "What are you going to do? Let Marvel take my place tomorrow?"

"No," he says. "That won't help."

"Then who?"

"I need to think. I'll talk to you later."

He hangs up the phone, and I feel tears prick at the back of my eyes. I stand there a minute, not wanting to turn back to Lila, but eventually I have no choice.

"I'm sorry," she says softly, after I hang up the phone. The doctor has given her something to make the pain stop. She just looks tired now. And terrified.

I go back to her bedside. "It's okay."

"No, it's not."

"Well—" I don't know what to say to her. "It is what it is, I guess."

Lila just nods, and I sit back in my chair.

I'm actually dozing off when she talks again. Her voice is barely above a whisper. "If I were you, I'd hate me."

I open my eyes and look at her. I have no idea how to respond to that. I can actually feel my jaw rusting shut this time. I open and close my mouth a couple of times and finally manage to say, "I don't hate you."

And it's true.

We've only been in California for one week, and I don't know Lila very well yet. I still want to go home to Denver. If I could, I'd go back to my house, to my school, my soccer team, my friends.

But I wasn't very happy before, either. I couldn't stop—

I look at the tray that's still sitting on the little table near my chair. Specifically, at the milk carton. I drank the milk, but it barely registered with me.

I didn't even look at the kid on the back of it.

I reach for the carton now. I turn it around and see a picture of a girl who is already in my collection.

"My dad is happy," I say, still looking at the girl. Laurel, who was on the back of the half-gallon when I first got to California. "I thought he would be sad forever."

Mrs. Norton comes in and interrupts whatever Lila was going to say. She takes Lila's blood pressure and checks on the baby with a stethoscope. She looks up at me and says, "Do you want to hear?"

I look at Lila and she nods, so I stand up. Mrs. Norton puts the stethoscope into my ears, and for a second everything is quiet. Then she taps the other end with her finger and after I nod to let her know I heard it, she puts the round part against Lila's belly.

At first it just sounds like a swish. Like the ocean, I think. It reminds me of being inside the clubhouse that first night. Then I hear a rhythm. A sort of *glub-glub-glub* that I think must be Lila's heart.

Mrs. Norton moves the stethoscope around, and then suddenly, there it is. So fast and light. It gallops, and it sounds so strong, I think that even if it's too early, anything with a heartbeat like that has to be a fighter. I take the earpieces out and hand them to Lila.

She takes them, slowly. There's a little monitor beside her that shows the baby's heartbeat as a jagged line, but it's not the same as hearing it.

"It's okay," I say.

She puts the earpieces into her ears, and Mrs. Norton shifts the round end. I see it in Lila's face, the moment when she hears the baby's heartbeat. She's beautiful again.

She finally takes the stethoscope out of her ears and hands them back to Mrs. Norton. "Thank you." Only she's looking at me, not the nurse.

Dad couldn't get a flight that left any earlier than noon the next day. I can't help the stab of disappointment. I do my best not to let it show, though.

Lila doesn't look well, and I doubt if she would have noticed my disappointment anyway. This is happening, the doctor said the last time he was in. They had hoped they could keep her from having the baby for a while, but now they don't think they can.

Whatever they gave her for the pain is not working anymore.

Lila grips my hand and pants through another contraction. "Oh God. Oh God. Oh God."

Mrs. Norton is off duty now, and the new nurse is named Alicia. At least she doesn't remind me of my mother. She has red hair that's cut short and is almost as tall as Lila.

She's checking Lila's blood pressure again when I hear a soft knock on the door.

"Hey, Tessa."

"Jay Jay?" I stand up. "What are you doing here?"

He gestures for me to come to the hallway. I look at Lila, and she says, "It's okay."

When I get to the door, Jay Jay grabs my hand and starts walking down the hall so fast I practically have to run to keep up.

"Wait a minute," I say, but he doesn't slow down. "Where are we going?"

He stops at a door and knocks on it three times fast, three times slow. It opens slowly at first, then Oscar throws it all the way open and pulls us into what turns out to be a staircase landing. Petey's there, too, but not Marvel.

I don't know how they got there, but I'm pretty sure they're there to yell at me for abandoning them tomorrow.

"I'm sorry," I say, before they can say anything. "Lila really needs me. My dad can't get here until tomorrow afternoon and her parents are on vacation and it's way too early for her to have the baby."

"Is she okay?" Jay Jay asks, just as Oscar opens his mouth.

"I think so," I say. "I heard the baby's—"

"Marv's in the hospital," Petey says, cutting me off.

"What?"

"He's here."

"Why?"

The boys all look at each other and Jay Jay finally says, "His arm is broken."

I exhale slowly. "Did he fall off his bike?"

"No, he didn't fall off his bike," Petey says. I take a step back from the anger in his voice. "We tried to sneak out to the clubhouse to figure out what we're going to do tomorrow, and she caught us."

Their mother does bad things to Marvel. That's what Jay Jay said. This time, she did a truly terrible thing to the little boy, and it was because I couldn't come to practice tomorrow. The stress of the last couple of hours backs up on me and tears run down my face. "I'm sorry. I'm so sorry."

"It's not your fault," Petey says, although Oscar is looking at me like it totally is my fault. Petey must notice that, too, because he adds, "It's not her fault."

"Is he going to be okay?"

"He's getting a cast," Petey answers. "He'll like that, at least. He'll want us to sign it."

We all laugh at that, but it's not happy laughter.

When it gets quiet again, I fidget a little and finally say what's on my mind. "Are you guys going to the community center tomorrow?"

"Well, we don't have Marvel *or* you now," Oscar says.

Jay Jay elbows Oscar. "Aaron called me this afternoon. He's going to practice with us."

It isn't fair for me to feel jealous. It was my choice to miss practice. And it was my idea for Aaron and his new crew to practice with them. That doesn't stop the little gut punch of envy, though. "Well, that's nice of him."

"Yeah," Oscar says. "Maybe it'll go so well, he can play with us in the finals."

I don't need this. "If you want him to, that's fine."

"Whatever! It's not like we're going to *win* either way. We never thought we were going to even make it this far."

"Jeez, O," Petey says.

"Look. We'll open the lemonade stand again next weekend. Either way, there will be enough money." Jay Jay looks at Oscar. "Thanks to Tessa."

"I can practice the rest of the week, and I'll be at the tournament."

"What about the lemonade stand?" Oscar asks.

"Definitely." I'm not sure, though, and it shows in my voice. What if Lila is still in the hospital with the baby?

"She thinks," Oscar says.

"Hey. It was her idea. And I'll feel better knowing she's at the hospital with Marv anyway," Petey says.

"I'll visit him." I can do that much, anyway. But again, as soon as I speak, I have another thought. "Will your mom be here?"

I hate asking that. It makes me sick, bringing her up. Petey's face tightens, and Oscar puts an arm around him. It's Jay Jay who answers. "She's here now."

"Doesn't anyone know she broke Marv's arm?"

Petey shakes his head firmly. "The last time we tried to tell, it made things worse."

Jay Jay said they went to separate foster homes. Is that worse than their mother breaking Marvel's arm?

"Stay out of her way," Petey says. "If you see her, just stay out of her way."

"Grandma will be back for Oscar and me pretty soon," Jay Jay says. "We'll come up and say goodbye before we go. She'll want to check on Lila."

"What floor is he on?" I ask.

"Fifth floor." Petey opens the staircase door. "I need to get back up there."

I want to stay with them. If we're all together, maybe we can cast some kind of spell that will keep Marvel safe. Some protective spell against his mother and against the mean things that she does to him. If we're together, Marvel will be okay.

But Lila needs me. And anyway, it feels like I'm being dismissed. "Okay. I'll be in Lila's room."

FOURTEEN

Alicia brings me a pillow and a blanket at about ten o'clock. I'm so tired, but there is no way I can sleep. Between Marvel on the fifth floor and Lila panting and moaning in the bed, and the sharp fear that it really is too early for the baby to be born, I am as wide awake as I've ever been.

"Thanks," I say.

Alicia smiles at me, but her attention is already on Lila. "Sweetheart, I need to examine you, to see if you're dilating."

That's my cue. I stand up and go out into the hallway.

The elevator is down the hall. Marvel is only two floors above me. Jay Jay promised he'd come say goodbye before he left the hospital, but it's been hours and I haven't seen him. I wonder if maybe the boys are in the waiting room on the fifth floor.

I look back at Lila's door and decide I have time to check. "I'll be back in a minute," I call out.

I hear Lila say something that sounds like "Okay." It might just as easily have been another moan, but I take it as at least an acknowledgment that she knows I'm taking a walk.

I ride the elevator up to the fifth floor. It looks pretty much exactly like the third floor. A nurse station across from the elevator and a hallway of room doors leading in either direction. The nurse at the station is a man. He's barely taller than me, with black hair and dark eyes that smile even though his mouth doesn't when he says, "Can I help you?"

"Is there a waiting room?" I ask.

He points behind him and to the right. "Down that hall."

"Thanks."

I think about asking for Marv's room or whether or not his mother is still there, but I don't want to get into trouble for wandering around the hospital alone. I might not be able to come back to see him later if I do.

The nurse turns back to his work and doesn't wait to see if I follow his directions. I bite my lip, then make a decision. I go back to the elevator first, pretending like I've changed my mind about the waiting room. When the nurse still doesn't look at me, I head down the hallway to my left.

Each door has a little glass window in it. I try to look casual as I peek through them one at a time.

Being in the hospital is strange. This floor is different from the one where babies are born. The smell, even all the way in California, is the same as the smell of the hospital in Denver where my mother died. Like a janitor just mopped the floors after someone was sick.

The dull quiet is the same, too. No one is paying attention to me, because everyone is so caught up in their own reasons for being here. No one speaks with their full voice. No one laughs. Even the televisions are on low.

Being in the hospital hits me hard all of a sudden. I remember curling up in a ball in a chair in Mom's room, wishing as hard as I could that she'd get better. I remember the moment when I knew that my wishing didn't work.

An old woman sits in her bed, watching the news. A teenage girl is in the other bed with her leg in a cast, hoisted up by a chain above her bed. Late as it is, her parents are there with a little boy that must be her brother.

A man is asleep in the next room. His hair is white on the white pillowcase, and his face shows pain even in his sleep. There isn't anyone in the room with him.

When I look through the little window into the third room, I see two men about my dad's age. They're both half sitting, half lying, staring straight ahead like maybe they can ignore each other and they'll magically find themselves back at home.

In the fourth room, I can't see the patient. A blond woman is sitting between the bed and the door. She's leaning over with her head on one folded arm, resting on the mattress. I almost move on, but something catches my eye.

Marvel's backpack is on the chair by the window. The woman must be his mother. She's petting him with her free hand, like a cat.

I take a step back, my heart in my throat, and bump into a nurse who's pulling a portable blood-pressure machine behind her.

"Coming in?" she asks.

I shake my head, duck around her, and try to force myself not to run back to the elevator.

✳ ✳ ✳

Lila is in pain when I get back to the third floor. I hear her in the hallway, not quite screaming, but definitely hurting. Her door is open, and there's a bustle of activity around it.

A nurse backs out of the room, pulling the bed with Lila in it.

"What's wrong?" I stand against a wall, out of the way. "What's happening?"

"We're having a baby." Alicia comes out behind the bed and offers me a smile that doesn't really reassure me. "We can't wait any longer."

Lila reaches for me, and I take her hand. I have to walk beside the bed because Alicia and the other nurse do not slow down.

"They're going to do a C-section," Lila says.

Her fingers grip mine hard, and I have to keep myself from pulling back. "What's that?"

"Surgery," she says. "The baby . . ."

"It's going to be okay," Alicia says. "There's a waiting room three doors down to your left. I'll come find you there as soon as I can."

"I have to stay with her," I say.

"You can't." Alicia doesn't leave any room for argument. I've heard that nurse voice enough times from my own mother to know there's no point in arguing.

It actually calms me. Alicia knows what she's doing.

The nurse at the head of the bed pushes a button and a door opens. They're gone before I can say anything else.

The waiting room has two families in it. They sit on either side, like little islands. One side has three sleepy little kids and grandparents, a giant stuffed bear, and a bouquet of balloons. The other has a young man, maybe Lila's age, sitting between an older man and woman. He's clutching a bunch of yellow roses in his hands, and I wonder if his wife is having a C-section, too.

I sit in a chair in the middle, because I don't want to impose on either family. I wish I had money to buy roses or balloons. Something.

The baby should have been born in August. It's at least six weeks early. I don't know what that means. I wish Alicia would come tell me. The longer I sit there, the more clearly I imagine the nurse coming to tell me that my new sister or brother is sick. Or worse. Or that Lila . . .

"Christine Adams." I pull my feet up to the edge of my chair and hug my legs as I whisper, murmuring into my knees. "Craig Alphonse. Richard Carlson. Elizabeth Dixon."

I make my way through all fifty-eight kids in my box. A little jolt of anxiety makes me feel like I might be sick. Did I remember them all? What if I missed one? What if missing one means that something bad will happen to Lila or the baby?

"Christine Adams. Craig Alphonse. Richard Carlson. Elizabeth Dixon," I start again, this time counting on my fingers as I go.

Forty-nine. That can't be right. I've forgotten nine names? Nine? I don't even know which ones are missing. I didn't stumble. I've gone through these names so many times, I should know them. Now I've forgotten nine of the kids in my box and tonight

I almost threw a milk carton away without even checking the back of it.

I'm in the middle of this thought when Alicia comes and sits next to me. "You have a brother," she says.

I swallow a hiccup, choking back tears that hadn't fallen yet. "Already?"

"It can happen fast," she says. "She didn't need a C-section after all."

"But the baby was a girl."

Alicia shakes her head. "A beautiful little boy. Very small, but he's a fighter, I can tell."

"You can?"

"Oh yeah. I've been doing this a long time. Your brother is strong."

"You should see his bedroom," I say. All that doll wallpaper and pink paint.

Alicia smiles and stands up again. "I just wanted to make sure you knew."

"Can I see him?"

She shakes her head. "Not yet. But Lila will be back in her room in a bit. You can wait for her there if you want to. I'll take you to the nursery as soon as you can see him."

I have a brother. I wonder if he has brown hair like me and dad, or if he's blond like Lila. The clock over the door says it's after eleven, and thinking about blond little boys makes me think about Marvel again.

I'm pretty sure that Jay Jay and Oscar left without saying goodbye. I didn't see Petey in Marvel's room, so I don't know where he is. It's late to call anyone, but when I get back to Lila's room, I decide to see if I can reach Jay Jay.

If his grandmother answers, I'll just hang up.

The room is weird now, without the bed in it. Too big and empty, with just the monitoring equipment and tables taking up space. I pick up the phone from the little table against the wall and dial Jay Jay's number.

He picks up before the first ring finishes. "Hello?"

"Hey," I say. "It's Tessa."

"Oh." I can't decide if he sounds upset or relieved. "How's Lila?"

"She had the baby. It's a boy."

"Are they okay?"

I want to say *Yes*. I want to believe that. But I don't know. "The nurse sounded like everything was pretty good."

"My grandma made me and Oscar leave without going to see you. She said it wasn't appropriate until after the baby. Petey's supposed to call, but I haven't heard from him."

"I don't think he's here," I say.

"Why not?"

"I saw . . . I think I saw his mother and there was someone in the bed. But Petey wasn't there."

"How do you know it was his room?"

"Marvel's backpack was there," I say.

Jay Jay makes a sound at the back of his throat.

When he doesn't say anything, I ask, "Do you think I should go see if I can find Petey?"

"Yeah. Call me back either way, okay?"

I hang up and then stand there a minute, staring at the phone. I pick it up again. I'm not sure whether the number I dial will work, it's long distance. But I dial anyway.

It rings several times before I finally hang up. It's Mountain Time in Denver. Nearly midnight. Gran is probably asleep.

I feel guilty, leaving Lila's room. What if they bring her in and I'm not here? I want to ask Alicia how long it will be, but I don't see her. I hesitate at the elevator before I push the up button.

Chances are that Petey is in the room now with his mother and Marvel. She wouldn't have gone home and left Petey at the hospital. Would she?

I honestly don't know. When I saw her before, and I'm pretty sure it was her, she seemed like a normal mom. Worried about her son. Upset, maybe, that he was hurt.

I am positive that Petey would not leave his mother alone in the hospital with Marvel if he had a choice.

She broke his arm. Petey couldn't stop whatever happened. The doctors must not think it was anything more than a little boy falling off his bicycle or something, because otherwise she wouldn't have been alone with him.

As the elevator takes me up to the fifth floor, I wish Dad were here. I would tell him. He'd know what to do. Or Mom. She would take care of Marvel. She'd make sure he was safe.

She would never let his mother hurt him again.

Maybe I should tell Alicia, I think as the door opens.

I go back to the room where I saw Marvel's backpack and the

woman leaning over the bed. This time, I know for sure that it's the right room. Marvel is lying in the bed, staring up at the ceiling. His left arm is in a cast from his hand over his forearm.

He won't play foosball for the rest of the summer.

He's alone in the room. I look behind me, both ways down the hall, and there isn't anyone. So I open the door and go in. "Marv?"

He turns to look at me, and I see a flash of fear across his small face before he recognizes me. "Tessa, what are you doing here?"

I go to the side of the bed. "How are you?"

"You shouldn't be here."

"I told Jay Jay I'd check on you."

"What are you doing at the hospital?"

"Lila had the baby. It's a boy."

"You really shouldn't be here." Marvel looks past me at the door. "You have to go."

"Where's Petey?"

"Mom took him to the cafeteria."

I feel a sharp ache in my stomach. "She's coming back?"

"Yes." He sounds miserable. Scared and in pain. I think that must be what the kids in my shoebox sound like, anytime they speak.

"What happened, Marvel?"

"I fell off my bed."

"What?"

"I fell off my bed, okay?"

I can't imagine what his mother did to him, to break his arm. I whisper, "I want to tell Lila's nurse. She's real nice. She'll help you."

Marvel sits up straighter, then whimpers because it must have hurt to move. "You have to go, Tessa."

But I can't just leave him there alone. "I don't know what to do."

"They'll put me in foster care," Marvel says, so low I can barely hear him. "It'll be worse, and I won't have Petey."

"You might be together."

"It will be worse. You promised."

"But, Marv . . ."

Before I can finish the door opens. I turn, half expecting to see Alicia, even though she works on the third floor and wouldn't have come all the way up here looking for me.

Petey and Marvel's mother is young. Older than Lila, of course, but much younger than my parents. For a split second, she looks at me with an absolutely blank stare. Like she's empty on the inside. And then her blue eyes narrow, and she says, "Who are you?"

I turn back to Marvel. I want to do something. I *have* to do something, but I don't know what. He shakes his head once, barely, and his blue eyes are the opposite of empty. They beg me to leave. To go and not tell anyone.

I turn back to his mother. Her face tightens a little, like she is anticipating something.

"Wrong room," I say. "I'm sorry."

Her eyebrows lift, but she doesn't say anything else when I scoot around her, out the door, and take off nearly running down the hallway toward the elevator.

By the time the elevator drops me back off on the third floor, I'm crying. Not just quiet tears either. I'm sobbing. I need to find a bathroom so I can pull myself together before I go back to Lila's room.

"Tessa?" I look up and see Alicia holding a clipboard, one hand on a doorknob. "Are you okay?"

I shake my head. The entire story is on the tip of my tongue, about to spill out, when she comes to me and puts a hand on my shoulder.

"Poor girl. Lila's fine. The baby needs a little help, but he's strong, just like I told you."

I exhale slowly. "Lila's back in her room?"

"I just left her there."

"Thank you." I really need a bathroom to at least wash my face before I see her.

"Here, let me take you. You'll see, she's just fine."

Before I can do or say anything else, she's holding my arm and walking me down the hall to Lila's room. I can't think of a way to make her stop without actually letting the whole story come out, right there in the hallway, so when she opens the door and waits for me to go in, I do.

"Tessa?" Lila is sitting up in her bed, propped up with pillows behind her. I take a gasping breath. "A boy. I can't believe it."

I'm too tired and confused to read her face. "There's nothing wrong with boys," I finally say.

She tilts her head. "I know that."

"You shouldn't have put up all that stupid wallpaper when you didn't know for sure."

"Tessa?" Lila winces as she sits herself up a little higher in her bed. I can't catch a good breath. I try, but it doesn't work. "Oh, Tessa. I don't care that the baby's a boy. It was silly of me to decide I knew."

"Are you okay?" I finally ask. "Are you going to be okay?"

"I'm fine. Tired, but I'm okay. The baby's small, but he's perfect, Tessa. I can't wait for you to see him."

I turn to look at Alicia, and she nods in agreement.

Now I am crying for more than just Marvel and Petey. I move without knowing that I'm going to and wrap my arms around Lila's neck. Instead of an awkward half pat, which is probably what I'd do, she holds me close.

"It's okay," she says, just like she did at the house before we got in the cab. "It's okay. It's okay."

"Tessa," Alicia says behind me. "Lila's still recovering."

I stand up, my face still messy with tears and now red with embarrassment. "I'm sorry."

"It's okay," Lila says again. I think she means it.

"Ring if you need me," Alicia says before going back out into the hall.

Lila's head is tilted, looking up at me like she can see right through me. Mom could do that. Dad could, too, when I was younger, but he hasn't in a long time. It makes me squirmy to get that look from her.

"What's wrong?" she finally asks.

I mean to say, *Nothing.* Or pretend it's just worry about her and the baby. I mean to re-rust my jaw. But what comes out is, "My friend Marvel is here, on the fifth floor."

"Marvel?"

"Yeah."

"Is he a friend of Jay Jay's?" she asks.

"His brother, Petey, is our age. Marv's seven."

"I remember Petey from the tournament," she says. "Marvel's the little boy in the bear costume?"

I nod, and I feel the tears welling up behind my eyes again. "He's our mascot."

"Why is he in the hospital?" she asks.

I promised. They will hate me. All of them. If I tell, they will hate me. But I remember the empty look in their mother's eyes when I left the room. I think about Marvel alone with her two floors up and I can't stop the words. "His mother broke his arm."

Lila's eyes open wider. "What?"

I cover my mouth with my hands. I want to take it back, but those aren't words you can unsay.

"Tessa?"

I just look at her. My jaw has truly rusted shut now. One minute too late. I couldn't tell her more if I wanted to. What I want to do is beg her not to tell anyone. And also beg her to send Alicia upstairs to make sure that Marvel is okay and that his mother isn't hurting him again because she found me in his room with him.

Lila waits until it's pretty obvious that I'm not going to talk and then says, "I'll ask a couple of questions, and you just shake your head yes or no, okay?"

I nod.

"Marvel's here in the hospital right now with a broken arm?"

I nod.

"His mother broke his arm?"

I nod.

"You're sure?"

My face crumbles as tears fall down my cheeks. I nod.

"Is she here with him?"

I nod.

"Okay." She looks at me another minute. "Do you want to see the baby?"

That one surprises me, and my jaw loosens up enough for me to ask, "Can I?"

"I think so." She reaches for the red button on the side of her bed and pushes it.

"Yes, Mrs. Hart?" a voice says, coming through a speaker somewhere near Lila.

"Would it be okay if my daughter walks down to the nursery to see the baby?"

Hearing her say *daughter* shakes me up. No one would believe it. I'm too old to be her daughter. And it's not true anyway. She should have said *stepdaughter*, but for some reason I'm glad she didn't. I don't know what to think, and I'm all caught up in that when the nurse says, "That would be fine."

"The nursery is down the hall, past the nurses' station," Lila says to me.

"Does he have a name?" I ask.

"It was supposed to be Joanna. I never even told your dad."

"You didn't?"

She shakes her head. "Maybe the baby will tell you his name when you see him."

I still feel tears welling up behind my eyes. "Maybe."

"Let me know."

✳ ✳ ✳

I walk down the hallway, toward the nurses' station. When I reach it, Alicia is on the phone. She looks at me as I walk past and hangs up the receiver.

"Want me to help you find the nursery?"

I shake my head. I need to do this alone. "No, thank you."

"All right then."

The nursery is behind a wall of windows. The older couple and the young man I saw in the waiting room are standing at one. A nurse is on the other side of the glass, holding up a baby wrapped in pink. The man has his arms around his waist, and I think he looks like he might fall over. The older man must think so, too, because he puts an arm around him.

"She's beautiful," the woman says. "Just perfect."

I think she kind of looks like a splotchy, squished-up prune, but I don't say so. That would be rude. Grandparents have to think their granddaughters are beautiful. And anyway, who knows what my new brother looks like.

There is a row of babies in the nursery. Each one is wrapped in either a blue or pink blanket, lying in a clear plastic baby bed. There's a card at the foot of each one with the words *Baby Boy* or *Baby Girl* and a last name.

The nurse puts the baby she's holding into a little bed with a card that says *Baby Girl Marshall*. I want to ask what they're going to name her, but that would be rude, too. And if they ask what my brother is named, I won't be able to tell them.

I look for a sign that says: "Baby Boy Hart." I walk down the row of windows, reading each one off under my breath. Even the girl ones. When I get to the end, the door opens. A nurse is there.

She's young and pretty with a name tag that says *Olivia*.

Olivia. It seems like bad luck to have a nurse with the name of Oscar's dead sister taking care of the baby.

"Can I help you?"

I almost can't tell her why I'm there. My jaw threatens to rust again, but I decide it is even worse luck not to see him. "I think my little brother's in there. Baby Boy Hart."

"What's your name?" she asks.

"Theresa Marie Hart." My cheeks burn immediately. Why did I give her my entire name?

Olivia smiles. "You'll have to come in to see him."

She goes into the nursery, but before I can follow her she comes back with a pair of blue paper booties for me to put over my shoes, like she has over hers. While I do that, she unfolds a matching robe.

She holds it open, and I slide my arms into it. After she ties it up in back, she says, "Almost done."

She covers my nose and mouth with a mask that hooks behind my ears and stretches a shower-cap-looking thing over my hair.

"Ready?" she asks.

I nod. If I need all this just to see him, I'm afraid my brother won't look like a prune. He'll look worse than that. What if I get scared? What if I do something awful that I can't take back, like run away or scream? Even if he never knows, I will.

Olivia leads me past the row of babies in their little plastic beds. There wasn't any sound in the hall, but in here you can hear a baby cry and others making snuffling noises.

I close my eyes when she leads me to another plastic bed. This one has a cover. Like the baby inside is in a bubble.

"Here we are," she says.

I force my eyes to open, and when I do, the relief makes my knees weak. He is beautiful. Just perfect. Even with a fine fuzz of blond hair covering not just his head, but his arms and legs and face, too.

He seems half the size of the baby girl Olivia held up for her dad and grandparents to see, but still perfect.

He's sleeping. I see his chest rise and fall as he breathes. He's wearing only a tiny diaper. There are things attached to him, to his head and his arm.

"Is he okay?" I ask.

"He's very small," Olivia said. "He'll have to stay here for a while. But he's breathing well. You should have heard him scream when we put the IV in."

I change my mind. She's not bad luck. Not at all. "I wish I could hold him."

"You'll be able to before you know it."

"Are his eyes brown or blue?"

"His are brown. Just like yours."

* * *

After a few minutes, we go back to the door of the nursery and Olivia takes my slippers and gown and mask. "Do you have other brothers and sisters?"

"I'm an only child. I mean, I was an only child."

She looks at me, like she's really analyzing me from top to bottom. Then, like she's learned something important, she nods and says, "You're going to be an excellent big sister, Theresa Marie Hart."

"Tessa," I say. "Everyone calls me Tessa."

"You are going to be an excellent big sister, Tessa."

FIFTEEN

Instead of dropping the ball for the next game, Denny bounces it off the field so it plonks me in the center of my forehead. Megan's across from me, her hands on the offense controls.

"Great," she says. "Now you have a third eye."

✳ ✳ ✳

"Tessa."

I sit up and rub the spot in the center of my forehead, expecting to find a lump, but the pain from my dream is gone.

I look up, then down again when I notice a balled-up piece of paper in my lap. I pick up the paper and look at the door again. "Jay Jay? What are you doing here?"

"Like you don't know."

He's angry. I don't know him well, but I don't need a third eye to see that he's truly pissed off. "What's wrong?"

He shakes his head, his lips pressing tight together.

I remember, suddenly, where I am. I look at Lila, asleep in her bed, then back at Jay Jay. "Is Marvel okay?"

"No, he's not okay." Jay Jay looks behind him and moves away from the door to make room for his grandmother, who walks in and directly to Lila's bed.

"Lila?" I say. I go to her bed and shake her foot. "Lila!"

She opens her eyes, tries to sit up, then stops with a moan.

"Don't hurt yourself," Mrs. Sampson says. She reaches for the little panel on the edge of the bed and pushes the button that raises the head. "There we go."

Lila isn't looking at Mrs. Sampson, though. She's looking at me, standing at the foot of her bed. "I'm sorry, Tessa."

"You told."

She takes a breath. "I did what I hope someone would do if they found out you were in trouble."

"You told." I look up at Mrs. Sampson, whose expression doesn't change, then I head for the door, staying as far from the old woman as I can. I have to push past Jay Jay, though.

He lets me go, but instead of staying in the room, he follows me. His long legs don't have any trouble keeping up.

"Where are you going?" he asks.

"To check on Marvel."

"Yeah," he says. "Maybe there's still time."

I stop then. Jay Jay watches me with his one blue eye and one green eye. "Time before what?"

He runs his tongue over his teeth and puts his weight on one foot and then the other. Finally, he must make some kind of decision, because he takes off again. "Come on."

I look back at Lila's door. Mrs. Sampson doesn't come after us. I don't think Lila could if she wanted to. I don't know what else to do, so I follow Jay Jay. He pushes the button for the elevator.

"What time is it?" I ask.

"Almost two in the morning." Jay Jay waits for the door to close once we're inside and says, "I heard Grandma taking Lila's call. While she was getting dressed, I called Oscar and he called Petey."

I wait for more, but he doesn't say anything else. "What did you mean? Time for what?"

He still doesn't say anything. He doesn't trust me anymore, and I don't blame him.

"They're running away," I say. "Aren't they?"

Still nothing, but I see it in his eyes.

"I don't understand. What about the tournament? They can't leave without the money."

And then I remember Marvel's backpack, sitting on the chair in his room. And I remember him putting the lunch box full of money into it. "The lemonade money. Marvel has it in his backpack."

"Are you going to go tell?" he asks.

"Oh my God." As soon as what he's saying sinks in, though, it doesn't make sense. "But why aren't the police here? The police show up for missing kids."

"I'm sure they'll be here."

The elevator door opens, and we walk out of it. We start toward Marvel's room, but the nurse at the station stops us. "Can I help you kids?"

My heart falls into my stomach. Before I can even try to say anything, though, Jay Jay says, "We're just visiting a friend."

The nurse looks at his watch, then back at us. "What's your friend's name?"

We look at each other, then back to him. Jay Jay finally says, "Marvel Lewis."

The nurse picks up the phone but doesn't take his eyes off us. "Stay right there."

I'm going to be sick. I look back at the elevator, wondering if I can call it again and get downstairs before the nurse can stop me.

The nurse speaks softly into the phone. My heart is pounding too hard for me to hear him, but he holds a finger up to us and it roots me in my spot.

Jay Jay pushes the elevator button.

"Young man!" The nurse stands up, but he still has the phone to his ear.

The elevator opens immediately. It's still there from when Jay Jay and I rode it up. We look at each other, then get into it. Jay Jay hits the third floor and then bounces his finger on the Close Doors button until it works.

"Holy crap," he says. "Oh my God."

"What was that?"

"They must know that Marvel is gone."

It takes everything in me to walk calmly back to Lila's room when the elevator gets to the third floor, instead of sprinting. Her door is open, and I stop so suddenly when I come to it that Jay Jay bangs into my back and makes me stumble forward.

A police officer stands at Lila's bed, next to Mrs. Sampson. He turns to look at us, and Lila says, "Tessa, there you are."

"Joshua," Mrs. Sampson says. "Come here."

He does, looking at me as he passes. We are in so much trouble.

But at that moment, I don't care. Because standing just to the side of the door, looking confused and out of place, is my gran.

I don't even care what she's doing there or how she got there. I throw myself into her arms, and she pulls me into her.

"Do you know where Peter and Marvel Lewis are?" Mrs. Sampson asks Jay Jay.

I turn my head and Jay Jay tries to turn to me, but his grandmother takes his arm and keeps his attention on her. He lets out a breath and says, "No, ma'am."

"Are you telling me the truth?" She looks at him like she can see right inside him. Like she would know if he lied.

Lila reaches a hand out to me as Jay Jay says, "I am telling you the truth."

I walk behind his grandmother to Lila's bed, bringing my own gran with me.

"What do you know, Tessa?" Lila asks quietly.

I take a breath and look at Jay Jay. He chews on his bottom lip but finally nods. I look at Gran and say, "We had a lemonade stand yesterday."

SIXTEEN

The baby's name is Jonathon Trevor Hart. Jack, for short.

Lila came home after three days, but Jack had to stay at the hospital, in his little bubble bed.

Gran came to California because my dad called her when he couldn't get an earlier flight. She came to take care of me. She ended up taking care of Lila, too, which should have been awkward and weird, but wasn't really.

Lila's mother and father are still in Jamaica. They sent flowers.

After a week Gran went home. No one says anything about Petey and Marvel anymore. I haven't seen Jay Jay and Oscar. I tried to. Twice. Both times Mrs. Sampson told me to go home. *Give them some time.*

I told. First Lila and then Gran and the men in Lila's room, and then when Dad finally got there, I told him. I told everything. I don't know what Jay Jay meant when he nodded at me, but based on the fact that he will not even speak to me now, he didn't mean for me to tell them everything.

Once I started speaking, I couldn't stop the words from spewing out of me. I told them about the lemonade stand. I told them about the foosball tournament. I told them about how Petey and Marvel's mother was mean to Marvel. I told them about the limp and that she broke his arm.

I will never forget the way Jay Jay looked at me when I finally stopped.

He looked at me like I was a traitor.

And now I can't even apologize, because he won't speak to me. And if he won't, then Oscar sure won't.

"Hey, Cookie."

I've been staring at Jay Jay's Aunt Lucy's bedroom window, like maybe I can will him to leave me a message in the panes. I finally look away. My dad's standing in my doorway. "Hi."

"We're going to the hospital. Why don't you come with us?"

I shrug. "I kind of just want to watch TV."

He comes closer to me and brushes my hair off my forehead. "Your friends are going to be okay."

Dad doesn't lie to me, but we both know that he can't know whether or not that's true. There's a shoebox in my headboard cubby full of kids who are not okay. And maybe, one of these days, I'll find Petey's and Marvel's pictures on the back of a milk carton. "You can't know that."

Dad smiles sadly. "You can believe this, Tessa. You did the right thing."

"Telling didn't help anything. Petey and Marvel are still gone. And now everyone hates me."

"No one hates you."

He's wrong. "Can I stay here while you go to the hospital?"

"I think so."

"Thanks, Dad."

He leaves me in my room and goes downstairs. Through the vent in my floor, I hear him talk to Lila, but I don't try to make out what they are saying.

Their door closes, and I hear their footsteps down the stairs, and then for the first time ever I'm alone in the house.

I reach for my shoebox and take the top off. I haven't looked at my missing kids since Jack was born. Not once. I haven't even noticed a milk carton.

It's weird to realize that for a few days, I've pretty much forgotten about them.

"Christine Adams," I whisper as I look at each card. "Craig Alphonse. Richard Carlson. Elizabeth Dixon."

I thought maybe they'd make me feel better. Less alone. Less lonely. But I can hardly focus on them. I try to remember Christine Adams's birthday or where she lived, but I have to look.

"This is the last time," I say. And this time it's true. If I want to, I can put my box away and never look at it again. Instead of being happy about that, though, I feel tears well up.

Gran has gone home to Denver. I don't have any friends. And now I don't have my lost kids, either. I don't need them. They never needed me. I pick up my box and go out on the balcony, into the beach air. The sun's low, but not enough that the sky's turning pink yet. I go down the stairs to the grass, then walk toward the bluff. When I get down the stairs, I sit on an upturned milk crate to think.

If Jay Jay and Oscar don't like that I'm in the clubhouse—they can come and tell me so themselves.

❋ ❋ ❋

"Jeez, Tessa. What are you doing here?"

I look up from the box in my lap, startled by Jay Jay's voice. How long have I been sitting here? I have to squint to see him in the almost dark. "I don't know."

"Well, your dad's been to my house looking for you. He's going to call the police soon, I think."

"I'll go home." Only, I don't move.

Jay Jay comes all the way into the clubhouse and sits on the milk crate next to mine. I can see him, but not clearly. Just like the first night that I was in California. "What's wrong?"

"Really?" I ask. "I have no friends. Petey and Marvel are probably dead in a ditch somewhere, even though I did tell."

"No, they're not."

I look up at him again. "What?"

He lifts one hip and reaches into his back pocket. "I got this today."

I take it from him. A postcard. The front says *Greetings from Detroit, Michigan.* Detroit is in big block letters with pictures of buildings in them. I turn it over and see handwriting that's more than just messy. It's lopsided and crooked. Like a kid writing with his wrong hand. "Marvel."

"Yeah."

Tell everyone we are ok with our uncle.
M + P

I turn the card over again, but there isn't any more message. "That's it?"

"That's it," Jay Jay says. "No return address or anything."

"They're afraid we'll tell."

"Or that my grandma might get to the mail before me."

I hold on to the card another minute, then slowly hand it back. "I'm sorry I told."

"I know."

"I didn't mean to. It's just—once I started, it all came out. I couldn't stop it."

"I know."

"But Oscar . . ."

"He knows, too."

"I'm really sorry," I say.

"I'm not. I think . . . I think we should have told sooner."

I look up at him. "You do?"

He shrugs one shoulder and looks uncomfortable, like his skin is a size too small. "I didn't think we'd win. I never really thought we'd get the money for them to leave."

"I didn't either," I say.

"I didn't think their mom would hurt Marvel like that. I knew . . . I knew she was mean to him, but I didn't know . . ."

Part of me wants to leave it there. Him not quite saying that he's forgiven me. Me not quite understanding what he thought was happening at Petey and Marvel's house. The chance that we might be friends again sometime feels so good. I'm afraid to ruin it by pushing my luck.

What if I say let's go to the community center tomorrow and he says forget it?

"The baby's name is Jack," I finally say. "He'll be in the hospital awhile, but the doctor thinks he's going to be okay."

"Grandma told me." Jay Jay scratches his head and then says, "Maybe I can come see him sometime."

And just like that, everything's okay again. Or at least, I know there is a chance that it will be. "Yeah. That would be good."

"So, what are you doing out here anyway? Your dad really is worried."

"I think I'm done." I look at the box in my lap. That I can even get those words out of my mouth is important. It means something. "I'm pretty sure I don't need these anymore."

"The milk cartons?" Jay Jay asks quietly.

"Yeah."

"Are you sure?"

"At the hospital, I almost threw one away without even looking. And then I *did* throw one away. I didn't even think about it. I didn't *try*, you know. I just threw away a milk carton."

"Like a normal person."

My face heats up. "Yeah."

"Do you want to keep them here?"

I'd thought about it. Maybe burying my box in the back of the clubhouse. Or setting up some kind of memorial altar to hold it. "I don't think I can keep them."

"Are you going to throw them away?"

No. "I don't think I can do that either."

We sit there for a while, without talking. It's Jay Jay who finally breaks the silence. "I have an idea."

He stands up and starts digging around in the big cooler that holds everything from marshmallows to comic books. There's some racket and then he makes a *eureka* sound and holds up a battered old cooking pan. The kind my mom used to make lasagna in. He dumps out a bunch of stuff that it's too dark for me to see.

I lift my eyebrows. "You want to *cook* them?"

"Kind of," he says. "But not quite."

"What are you talking about?"

He puts the baking pan on top of the grocery cart basket that the boys have used to house their bonfires and reaches back into the cooler. This time, he comes out with a comic book and starts to pull the pages apart, crumpling them up and putting them in the pan.

He doesn't look at me when he says, "When my grandpa died, my grandma put his ashes into the ocean."

"Oh." I don't know what else to say.

"Right here, in the bay," he says. "She hired a man with a boat to take us out and we just . . . we dumped him into the water."

"God," I whisper. "Was it awful?"

He looks up at me when the pan is full of crumpled comic book pages. "It was weird. But he loved the beach. I think he wanted it."

"They aren't dead, though," I say. "The kids on the pictures, I mean."

"Maybe my grandpa can look out for them anyway." Jay Jay

stands and reaches a hand down to help me up. It's a full moon outside, and the clubhouse is full of cool light. "Do you trust me?"

My stomach feels like it's full of ice, and my hands and feet are numb. I want to take my box and run away. But I don't have to.

❊ ❊ ❊

I wish that Mom was in the ocean, with Jay Jay's grandpa. She would look after these kids. She would keep them safe and help them to not be afraid.

I pick up my box and settle it carefully in the nest of comic book pages inside the pan.

Jay Jay finds a book of matches, and the dry pages go up so fast, it takes my breath away. There is no time for me to change my mind. The sides of the box blacken and curl and smoke.

"Christine Adams," I whisper. "Craig Alphonse. Richard Carlson. Elizabeth Dixon."

I say their names slowly, as the fire in the baking pan flares and the box ignites. All fifty-eight names. I remember every one of them and that feels good. Like a memorial service, almost.

"Camilla Sampson," Jay Jay says, next to me. When I look at him, his eyes are squeezed closed. "Joshua Marks."

"Your parents?"

He opens his eyes. The firelight flickers across his face. "They're missing. Just like those kids."

I watch the smoke flow out to the beach. We sit side by side on milk crates, waiting for the fire to burn itself out, until there is nothing but ashes in the bottom of the pan.

It's late, but I'm not tired. I feel like I might stay awake the rest of my life. Jay Jay pulls his T-shirt over his head and uses it like oven mitts, so he can lift the pan.

We are alone on the beach. There are people nearby, in the houses, including our own families. But right now, we are completely alone.

Jay Jay walks across the sand, toward the water. There is no dock out here, no way to get beyond the edge of the shore without wading in. We kick off our shoes by some kind of silent agreement and walk in until the water is lapping at our knees, dowsing the bottom edges of our shorts.

Christine Adams.

Craig Alphonse.

Richard Carlson.

Elizabeth Dixon.

I say their names again. One by one as Jay Jay tips the ashes into the water.

"Peter and Marvel," I say at the end. "Peter and Marvel Lewis."

"Camilla Sampson," Jay Jay says, louder this time, his face tipped up to the moon. "Joshua Marks. William Sampson."

William must be his grandfather, I think. I close my eyes and say, "Margaret Hart."

The water is cool enough to make my skin numb. I float a hand over the surface. In the dark, I can't see the ashes, but I know they are there.

ACKNOWLEDGMENTS

This is one of those stories that I dug straight out of my heart. It's set in the 1980s, when I was Tessa's age, in the house on the beach my dad and stepmother moved to just before my baby brothers were born.

I shared that cherry-on-the-cupcake room with my sisters and had a killer lemonade stand on the bluff.

So—thank you to Jill, Russel, Alison, Kevin, Austin, Kyle, Patrick, and Ryan—always.

Especially Jill, who was on my mind so much as I wrote this story that I kept seeing her everywhere I looked. And Kyle, who is my first reader and biggest fan.

And our dad, who filled that house with books and encouraged adventure (and still does). He taught me that doing the best you can is enough, and that's the lesson Tessa learns, too.

And my mom, who never, ever would have let me read *Flowers in the Attic* or have a lemonade stand on the beach. It was my stepmom who snuck that story to me the summer after seventh grade and bankrolled our enterprise.

Thank you to my friend David, who lent me his real-life hero mama, Kathleen, so that Tessa's mother could be something special. And for believing that I could find this story and do it justice.

Big, big love to Kevin, Adrienne, Nicholas, and Ruby for putting up with me when I'm deep in the storytelling trenches.

Also, Zach, who keeps my head screwed on straight.

And thank you to every single Ninja Writer for being my tribe.

Elizabeth Bennett, my incredible literary agent, had the dubious job of telling me at the beginning that this story wasn't working and then staying on the phone with me while I had a complete breakdown. She trusted that I could make it better and told me so as many times as I needed to hear it.

Thank you, Liz Szabla and the whole team at Macmillan, who helped make *Center of Gravity* real.